BASIL THOMSON

THE CASE OF NAOMI CLYNES

SIR BASIL HOME THOMSON (1861-1939) was educated at Eton and New College Oxford. After spending a year farming in Iowa, he married in 1889 and worked for the Foreign Service. This included a stint working alongside the Prime Minister of Tonga (according to some accounts, he *was* the Prime Minister of Tonga) in the 1890s followed by a return to the Civil Service and a period as Governor of Dartmoor Prison. He was Assistant Commissioner to the Metropolitan Police from 1913 to 1919, after which he moved into Intelligence. He was knighted in 1919 and received other honours from Europe and Japan, but his public career came to an end when he was arrested for committing an act of indecency in Hyde Park in 1925 – an incident much debated and disputed.

His eight crime novels featuring series character Inspector Richardson were written in the 1930's and received great praise from Dorothy L. Sayers among others. He also wrote biographical and criminological works.

Also by Basil Thomson

BASIL THOMSON

THE CASE OF NAOMI CLYNES

With an introduction by
Martin Edwards

DEAN STREET PRESS

Published by Dean Street Press 2016

All Rights Reserved

First published in 1934 by Eldon Press as
Inspector Richardson CID

Cover by DSP

Introduction © Martin Edwards 2016

ISBN 978 1 911095 71 2

www.deanstreetpress.co.uk

Introduction

Sᴉʀ Bᴀsɪʟ Tʜᴏᴍsᴏɴ's stranger-than-fiction life was packed so full of incident that one can understand why his work as a crime novelist has been rather overlooked. This was a man whose CV included spells as a colonial administrator, prison governor, intelligence officer, and Assistant Commissioner at Scotland Yard. Among much else, he worked alongside the Prime Minister of Tonga (according to some accounts, he *was* the Prime Minister of Tonga), interrogated Mata Hari and Roger Casement (although not at the same time), and was sensationally convicted of an offence of indecency committed in Hyde Park. More than three-quarters of a century after his death, he deserves to be recognised for the contribution he made to developing the police procedural, a form of detective fiction that has enjoyed lasting popularity.

Basil Home Thomson was born in 1861 – the following year his father became Archbishop of York – and was educated at Eton before going up to New College. He left Oxford after a couple of terms, apparently as a result of suffering depression, and joined the Colonial Service. Assigned to Fiji, he became a stipendiary magistrate before moving to Tonga. Returning to England in 1893, he published *South Sea Yarns*, which is among the 22 books written by him which are listed in Allen J. Hubin's comprehensive bibliography of crime fiction (although in some cases, the criminous content was limited).

Thomson was called to the Bar, but opted to become deputy governor of Liverpool Prison; he later served as governor of such prisons as Dartmoor and Wormwood Scrubs, and acted as secretary to the Prison Commission. In 1913, he became head of C.I.D., which acted as the enforcement arm of British military intelligence after war broke out. When the Dutch exotic dancer and alleged spy Mata Hari arrived in England in 1916, she was arrested and interviewed at length by Thomson at Scotland

Yard; she was released, only to be shot the following year by a French firing squad. He gave an account of the interrogation in *Queer People* (1922).

Thomson was knighted, and given the additional responsibility of acting as Director of Intelligence at the Home Office, but in 1921, he was controversially ousted, prompting a heated debate in Parliament: according to *The Times*, "for a few minutes there was pandemonium". The government argued that Thomson was at odds with the Commissioner of the Metropolitan Police, Sir William Horwood (whose own career ended with an ignominious departure fromoffice seven years later), but it seems likely be that covert political machinations lay behind his removal. With many aspects of Thomson's complex life, it is hard to disentangle fiction from fact.

Undaunted, Thomson resumed his writing career, and in 1925, he published *Mr Pepper Investigates*, a collection of humorous short mysteries, the most renowned of which is "The Vanishing of Mrs Fraser". In the same year, he was arrested in Hyde Park for "committing an act in violation of public decency" with a young woman who gave her name as Thelma de Lava. Thomson protested his innocence, but in vain: his trial took place amid a blaze of publicity, and he was fined five pounds. Despite the fact that Thelma de Lava had pleaded guilty (her fine was reportedly paid by a photographer), Thomson launched an appeal, claiming that he was the victim of a conspiracy, but the court would have none of it. Was he framed, or the victim of entrapment? If so, was the reason connected with his past work in intelligence or crime solving? The answers remain uncertain, but Thomson's equivocal responses to the police after being apprehended damaged his credibility.

Public humiliation of this kind would have broken a less formidable man, but Thomson, by now in his mid-sixties, proved astonishingly resilient. A couple of years after his trial, he was appointed to reorganise the Siamese police force, and he continued to produce novels. These included *The Kidnapper* (1933), which Dorothy L. Sayers described in a review for the *Sunday Times* as "not so much a detective story as a sprightly fantasia upon a detective theme." She approved the fact that Thomson wrote "good English very amusingly", and noted that "some of his characters have real charm." Mr Pepper returned in *The Kidnapper*, but in the same year, Thomson introduced his most important character, a Scottish policeman called Richardson.

Thomson took advantage of his inside knowledge to portray a young detective climbing through the ranks at Scotland Yard. And Richardson's rise is amazingly rapid: thanks to the fastest fast-tracking imaginable, he starts out as a police constable, and has become Chief Constable by the time of his seventh appearance – in a book published only four years after the first. We learn little about Richardson's background beyond the fact that he comes of Scottish farming stock, but he is likeable as well as highly efficient, and his sixth case introduces him to his future wife. His inquiries take him – and other colleagues – not only to different parts of England but also across the Channel on more than one occasion: in *The Case of the Dead Diplomat*, all the action takes place in France. There is a zest about the stories, especially when compared with some of the crime novels being produced at around the same time, which is striking, especially given that all of them were written by a man in his seventies.

From the start of the series, Thomson takes care to show the team work necessitated by a criminal investigation. Richardson is a key connecting figure, but the importance of his colleagues' efforts is never minimised in order to highlight his brilliance. In *The Case of the Dead Diplomat*, for instance, it is the trusty Sergeant Cooper who makes good use of his linguistic skills and flair for impersonation to trap the villains of the piece. Inspector Vincent takes centre stage in *The Milliner's Hat Mystery*, with Richardson confined to the background. He is more prominent in *A Murder is Arranged*, but it is Inspector Dallas who does most of the leg-work.

Such a focus on police team-working is very familiar to present day crime fiction fans, but it was something fresh in the Thirties. Yet Thomson was not the first man with personal experience of police life to write crime fiction: Frank Froest, a legendary detective, made a considerable splash with his first novel, *The Grell Mystery*, published in 1913. Froest, though, was a career cop, schooled in "the university of life" without the benefit of higher education, who sought literary input from a journalist, George Dilnot, whereas Basil Thomson was a fluent and experienced writer whose light, brisk style is ideally suited to detective fiction, with its emphasis on entertainment. Like so many other detective novelists, his interest in "true crime" is occasionally apparent in his fiction, but although *Who Killed Stella Pomeroy?* opens with a murder scenario faintly reminiscent of the legendary Wallace case of 1930, the storyline soon veers off in a quite different direction.

Even before Richardson arrived on the scene, two accomplished detective novelists had created successful police series. Freeman Wills Crofts devised elaborate crimes (often involving ingenious alibis) for Inspector French to solve, and his books highlight the patience and meticulous work of the skilled police investigator. Henry Wade wrote increasingly ambitious novels, often featuring the Oxford-educated Inspector Poole, and exploring the tensions between police colleagues as well as their shared values. Thomson's mysteries are less convoluted than Crofts', and less sophisticated than Wade's, but they make pleasant reading. This is, at least in part, thanks to little touches of detail that are unquestionably authentic – such as senior officers' dread of newspaper criticism, as in *The Dartmoor Enigma*. No other crime writer, after all, has ever had such wide-ranging personal experience of prison management, intelligence work, the hierarchies of Scotland Yard, let alone a desperate personal fight, under the unforgiving glare of the media spotlight, to prove his innocence of a criminal charge sure to stain, if not destroy, his reputation.

Ingenuity was the hallmark of many of the finest detective novels written during "the Golden Age of murder" between the wars, and intricacy of plotting – at least judged by the standards of Agatha Christie, Anthony Berkeley, and John Dickson Carr – was not Thomson's true speciality. That said, *The Milliner's Hat Mystery* is remarkable for having inspired Ian Fleming, while he was working in intelligence during the Second World War, after Thomson's death. In a memo to Rear Admiral John Godfrey, Fleming said: "The following suggestion is used in a book by Basil Thomson: a corpse dressed as an airman, with despatches in his pockets, could be dropped on the coast, supposedly from a parachute that has failed. I understand there is no difficulty in obtaining corpses at the Naval Hospital, but, of course, it would have to be a fresh one." This clever idea became the basis for "Operation Mincemeat", a plan to conceal the invasion of Italy from North Africa.

A further intriguing connection between Thomson and Fleming is that Thomson inscribed copies of at least two of the Richardson books to Kathleen Pettigrew, who was personal assistant to the Director of MI6, Stewart Menzies. She is widely regarded as the woman on whom Fleming based Miss Moneypenny, secretary to James Bond's boss M – the Moneypenny character was originally called "Petty" Petteval. Possibly it was through her that Fleming came across Thomson's book.

Thomson's writing was of sufficiently high calibre to prompt Dorothy L. Sayers to heap praise on Richardson's performance in his third case: "he puts in some of that excellent, sober, straightforward detective work which he so well knows how to do and follows the clue of a post-mark to the heart of a very plausible and proper mystery. I find him a most agreeable companion." The acerbic American critics Jacques Barzun and Wendell

Hertig Taylor also had a soft spot for Richardson, saying in *A Catalogue of Crime* that his investigations amount to "early police routine minus the contrived bickering, stomach ulcers, and pub-crawling with which later writers have masked poverty of invention and the dullness of repetitive questioning".

Books in the Richardson series have been out of print and hard to find for decades, and their reappearance at affordable prices is as welcome as it is overdue. Now that Dean Street Press have republished all eight recorded entries in the Richardson case-book, twenty-first century readers are likely to find his company just as agreeable as Sayers did.

Martin Edwards

www.martinedwardsbooks.com

Chapter One

THE CHARWOMAN of the flat on the first floor came tearing down the back stairs into the milk-shop panting and breathless.

"Come quick, Mrs. Corder, there's a terrible escape of gas upstairs. I just opened the door of my lady's flat and the gas drove me back. I didn't dare go in."

"Oh, my God! And not a man about the place! I'll come up with you. The first thing to do is to open the window and get the gas turned off. Come on; the shop'll have to mind itself."

Mrs. Corder caught up a towel as she went and the two women raced up the stairs. When they reached the top the smell of gas was overpowering, but Mrs. Corder held the towel over her mouth and ran to the door of the first floor flat. She was a woman of decision. She threw the door wide open and with her free hand flung back the shutters and threw up the window sash. Then she ran back into the passage to breathe.

"It's coming from the kitchen from the gas-oven," she gasped. "You stay here while I run in again and turn it off."

With the towel pressed against her face she made a second plunge into the poisoned air and emerged white and shaking.

"I've got it turned off, but oh! My God! Miss Clynes is lying in there with her head in the gas- oven."

"You don't mean it? Whatever made her do that? I suppose I'd better go out and find a policeman."

"No, you needn't do that. I'll ring up the police- station from the 'phone upstairs. You go and keep your eye on the shop a minute. Call me if I'm wanted."

Three minutes later Mrs. Corder returned to her shop. "The gas isn't so bad now. If we keep the shop door open the draught will blow it all out."

"I can't go up there by myself, Mrs. Corder; I wouldn't have the nerve."

"No one must go up there or touch anything until the police come. They're sending round a plain clothes officer, and they say that they've 'phoned the police surgeon, so we can't do any more till they come."

"Are you sure she's dead, Mrs. Corder?"

"She must be. No one could have lived through all that gas. Ah! Here's John at last! He'll go up."

A rosy, broad-shouldered man rolled into the shop and stopped short. "Why, what's up, Jenny? You look all scared."

"Miss Clynes has been and gassed herself, Mr. Corder," said the charwoman, who was beginning to enjoy herself, "and Mrs. Corder has been risking her life turning off the gas."

"Go up, John, and make sure she's quite dead. I'm sure I don't know what you do to bring people round when they've been gassed."

The husband turned to obey the order: she called after him, "Mind and not touch the body or anything else, more than you can help. The police are on their way down with the doctor. And you, Mrs. James; you mustn't go away. The police will want to question us all."

Annie James was thrilled to the marrow. "Will they? It's the very first time I've been mixed up in a suicide."

A heavy step was heard descending the stairs. John Corder, the roses faded from his cheeks, returned to the shop, shaking his head. "She's dead all right, poor lady—stone cold."

Two men darkened the shop door: the one a tall, broad-shouldered man approaching forty; the other a younger man with a professional air about him. He carried an attaché-case.

"Are you Mrs. Corder?" asked the first, addressing the mistress of the shop.

"Yes, sir."

"You telephoned to the station that a woman had been gassed in this house."

"That's right, sir. It's the lady that has the flat overhead. I suppose that you're the police inspector?"

"No, I'm Detective Sergeant Hammett. The detective inspector is on leave. This gentleman is Dr. Wardell, the police surgeon. Will you kindly show us the way upstairs?"

"This way, gentlemen. Shall I go first to show you?" said John Corder, leading the way.

Mrs. James, the charwoman, in a spasm of curiosity, would have followed if Mrs. Corder had not held her back.

The three men seemed to fill the little kitchen.

"Can we have a little more light?" asked the doctor.

"Certainly, sir." The dairyman switched on the electric light.

The doctor knelt down beside the body.

"We'll leave you, doctor," said the sergeant. "You'll find us in the next room when you want us. Now, Mr. Corder, I want a few particulars from you." They had moved into the bed-sitting-room. The sergeant looked round it and clicked his tongue. "Nicely furnished," he said. "The poor lady knew how to make herself comfortable."

"Oh, the furniture doesn't belong to her. She was only a sub-tenant."

The sergeant had taken out his notebook. "What was her name?"

"Miss Clynes; first name Naomi."

"Her age?"

"I couldn't tell you that. I should think by the look of her that she was between thirty and forty.

"How long had she been with you?"

"Let me see. It must be three months now."

"Do you know the address of any of her friends?"

"No, Sergeant, I don't. She was very reserved and we scarce ever saw her. You see, the flat has its own front door—

37A Seymour Street—just round the corner, and she had no occasion to come into the shop."

"But she must have had friends who called on her?"

"Funny you should say that. My wife was talking of that very thing less than a week ago—wondering whether she ever had any visitors."

"Was she regular with her rent?"

"I can't tell you that either. She took a sublease of the flat from Harding & Anstruther—the house-agents in Lower Sloane Street. It's them that receive the rent and pay it over to the real tenant."

"The real tenant?"

"Yes; you see we let the flat by the year to Mr. Guy Widdows, but he's travelling abroad most of the time, and then the house-agents let his flat for him by the month. He's out in Algeria now, and we forward his letters to him."

"Was she employed anywhere? What did she do with her time?"

"Oh, she was an authoress, I believe, but her charwoman you saw downstairs might be able to tell you more about that."

"I'll see her presently. Now tell me, who was sleeping on the premises last night?"

"No one but my roundsman, Bob Willis. He sleeps in that little room at the back of the shop."

"Where do you and your wife sleep?"

"We've got a room at 78 King's Road."

"Who has the floor above this?"

"It's an office of some Jewish society, but no one sleeps there. A girl clerk goes up there once or twice a week to open their letters, but that's all."

"Have they got a latchkey to the door in Seymour Street?"

"Yes, they have, otherwise they would have to come through my shop."

The doctor entered the room from the kitchen and addressed Sergeant Hammett. "It's a clear case of gas-poisoning, Sergeant. If you'll give me a hand we'll carry the body into this room."

"Very good, sir. Can you form any opinion about the hour when death took place?"

"Before midnight, I should say. At any rate the woman's wrist-watch stopped at 5.10, so she hadn't wound it up overnight."

"There is no trace of violence?"

"Not a trace, except a slight bruise on one of her wrists, but she might have got that in knocking it against the kitchen range. I shall know more when we get the body down to the mortuary. Now, if you'll come along."

The three men carried the body reverently into the bed-sitting-room and laid it out on the divan-bed. Corder was sent downstairs for a sheet to cover it, and to call Annie James, the charwoman, to answer Sergeant Hammett's questions.

"You'll report; the case to the coroner, sir?" said Hammett, "and, if you are passing the police-station, perhaps you will give the word for them to send along the ambulance to take the body to the mortuary."

"I will. I suppose that you'll be able to tell the coroner's officer when he comes where the woman's relatives are to be found. The coroner is always fussy about that."

"That's the trouble, sir. Nobody here seems to know that she had any relatives, or for the matter of that, any friends. She had no visitors, they say. Perhaps you'll mention this to the coroner when you ring him up. I'm going to inquire at the house-agent's on my way to the station."

"Then you are not going to search the flat?"

"No, doctor. I'm going to take a statement from the charwoman, and then I shall have to ask for help from Central. You see my inspector is away on leave, and I've more on my hands than I can do without this case."

Annie James, the charwoman, knocked at the door. The doctor nodded good-bye to the sergeant and stumbled down the dark staircase. The woman entered the room timidly and shook with emotion at the sight of her late employer lying pallid and still on the couch.

"Please, sir, I've brought the sheet."

"Then help me to cover her up."

"Oh, pore thing! Pore thing! It's awful to think of her being took like that, and that I shall never hear her voice again. So kind, she was, to me."

"I want you to sit down there and answer my questions. Is your name Annie James?"

"That's right, sir."

"And you used to do charing here for this lady, Miss Clynes?"

"That's right, sir. I got to know of her through an agency. She wanted a lady's help, and of course, knowing me as they did, they said, 'You couldn't do better than take Mrs. James—that is, of course, if she's free to oblige you, and...'"

"And she engaged you. How long ago was that?"

"Let's see: it must have been eleven or twelve weeks ago. I know it was ..."

"Did you find her cheerful and happy?"

"I wouldn't go so far as to say that, sir. She would pass the time of day with you, but she was never what you might call chatty. Very reserved and quiet I'd call her."

"Did she ever talk to you about her friends?"

"No, sir, not a word. And another thing I thought funny. She never had anyone to tea—at least I never saw more than one cup and plate used in the flat. She seemed to spend all her time tapping on her typewriter. She was so busy at it that sometimes she didn't seem to hear me when I spoke to her."

"She had letters, I suppose?"

"Very few that I know of, sir. Sometimes I used to see an envelope or two in the dustbin."

"Did she ever say what part of the country she came from?"

"No, sir. I did ask her once, but all I could get out of her was that she came somewhere from the north. She cut me quite short."

"But she didn't seem to you to be depressed—as if she had something on her mind?"

"No, sir. If she wasn't talkative, it was just her way, I think. Some are born like that, aren't they, sir?"

"And so it was a great surprise to you this morning to find that she had taken her own life?"

"Yes, sir. I can't tell you what a shock it's been."

"Thank you, Mrs. James. I have your address in case we shall want you again."

After calling on the house-agents in Lower Sloane Street, Sergeant Hammett took the Underground from Sloane Square to Westminster and sent in his name to the Chief Constable.

He was standing in the Central Hall when a gentleman of middle age, who appeared to be in a hurry, was stopped by the constable on duty and asked to fill up a printed form stating his name and his business.

"Nonsense! Everybody knows what my business is. I'm the coroner for the South Western district, and I want to see the Assistant Commissioner of the C.I.D. at once."

"Then please put that on the form, sir."

"This is quite new. I've never had to do this before."

"Those are the Commissioner's orders, sir. You can put on the form that you are in a hurry, sir."

"Oh, well, if those are your orders—there, but please see that the form goes to Mr. Morden at once. I've no time to waste."

The constable carried the form upstairs, and two minutes later returned with the Assistant Commissioner's messenger. "Please step this way, sir."

The coroner was conducted to a large room on the first floor where Charles Morden was sitting at his office table.

"You seem to be full of red tape since I was here last."

Morden laughed. "Yes, it's a new rule, but there is a useful side to it. What can I do for you?"

"My officer reported to me this morning that the Chelsea police had failed to find the address of any relations or friends of a woman who committed suicide last night by gassing herself. How can I hold an inquest with nothing but the medical evidence to go upon? It's absurd! The woman must have had friends somewhere."

"Let me see; the divisional detective inspector is away on leave, but the first-class sergeant ought to be working on the case."

He rang the bell for his messenger. "Find out whether Sergeant Hammett from B Division is in the building," he said. "Send him in if he is."

In less than a minute Hammett was ushered into the room.

"This is the officer in charge of the inquiry," said Morden to the coroner. "He will tell you how far he has got. The coroner wishes to know whether you have found any friends of the woman who gassed herself last night?"

"I've questioned everybody in the house, sir, and I think that they are telling the truth when they say that the woman received no visitors at her flat, and, as far as they know, received very few letters. I've called at the house-agents', and there I've got a little further. She was required to furnish two references before entering into possession. I have their names and addresses here." He took out his note-book. "A clergyman, the Vicar of St. Andrew's, Liverpool, and a Mr. John Maze, a solicitor of Liverpool. Both references were satisfactory: both were shown to me."

"Did you find any correspondence in her flat?"

"To tell you the truth, sir, I haven't had time to search it yet. Our hands are pretty full with that big burglary in Tedworth Square, and that shopbreaking case in Lower Sloane Street, and I came on here to ask for help over this case."

"Um! It seems, on the face of it, to be quite a simple case—one that the division ought to be able to clear up without calling in help from outside. Still—if you are really pressed—I'll see what can be done." He pressed a button on his table and picked up the receiver of his desk telephone.

"Is that you, Mr. Beckett? Is there an inspector free in Central to undertake a case?"

"..."

"Yes, he would do all right. Will you send him round?" Turning to Sergeant Hammett, he said,

"Inspector Richardson will take over the case. You'd better have a talk with him as you go out."

The coroner rose. "I suppose," he said, "that this inspector will get into touch with those people in Liverpool and let me know all that he finds out about the woman?"

"Yes, I'm sure he will."

"He's a good man?"

"About the best of the younger men; he'll make a name for himself some day: he has had very quick promotion."

Chapter Two

HAMMETT KNEW all about Inspector Richardson by repute. He was one of the first-class sergeants who imagined that they had a grievance against him because he had been promoted out of his turn, but Richardson was gradually overcoming this prejudice by his unfailing courtesy and good temper; indeed, very few of the malcontents bore him any ill will at this moment.

Hammett went to the inspectors' room and found him packing up stationery and instruments in his attaché-case.

"Mr. Morden has put you in charge of a case in my division, Mr. Richardson. He wants me to tell you how far we've got up to date."

"A case of suicide, Mr. Beckett said."

"So far as the police surgeon could say after his first examination of the body, it was an ordinary case of gas-poisoning."

"I fancy that you must be in a hurry to get back, Sergeant. We might take the Underground and talk as we go."

They walked across to the Westminster Underground Station and took up their seats at the end of a car where they were free from possible eavesdroppers.

"You say that the dead woman had a servant?" asked Richardson.

"Only a charwoman who came in for a couple of hours in the morning."

"Intelligent?"

"Too much so. She's one of those women who don't know how to stop talking until you pull them up. She's enjoying herself over this suicide, I can tell you."

"You say the deceased woman was an authoress?"

"So they told me at the milk-shop; at any rate she had a typewriter." He said no more until they were approaching Seymour Street. "Here we are, Inspector. This is the door by which the tenants upstairs went in and out."

The number—37A—was painted on the door. One stone step raised the floor from the street level. Richardson noticed that the step was whitened and that the keyhole and knocker on the green door were clean and polished, and so was the brass of the letter-box. There being no means of opening the door without the key, Hammett took Richardson round to the milk-shop and introduced him to the Corders.

"This is Inspector Richardson from New Scotland Yard, Mr. Corder. He'll have to have the run of the flat for a day or two."

"Very good, sir. While you were away the ambulance called and I helped the men to get the body down the stairs. There was quite a crowd outside to see it go off, and everyone stops to point out the house of the suicide, as they call it. It's a bit unpleasant for us."

"Oh, they'll soon forget all about it; there'll be some fresh attraction for them to-morrow. Now, Mr. Richardson, if you'll follow me I'll take you upstairs."

They climbed the back stairs and reached the flat, Hammett briefly explaining the general layout of the house as they went. "You see, if it was a case of murder or even burglary, one might suspect that this office upstairs where the door is never locked was used as a hiding-place by the guilty person, who might have got in unobserved when the shop was empty for a minute, but the police surgeon seems satisfied that it was a clear case of suicide by gas-poisoning. I shall be curious to hear whether you find any relations or friends; it seems extraordinary that a woman in fairly easy circumstances should have no one in the world related to her."

"I'll let you know, and now as you're a busy man, don't trouble to wait any longer: I'll get to work."

Richardson had his own way of searching a room. He took off and folded his coat and turned up his sleeves to the elbows. Then he turned the key in the door. His first step was to go over the entire surface of the floor with a reading-glass: very carefully he moved out the divan from the wall and examined the surface of the cork linoleum that lay under it. Here he made his first discovery. Half hidden under the fringe of the Oriental carpet he found a cigarette of an expensive make. He was not himself a connoisseur of cigarettes, but he noted two points about this one—that it was gold-tipped and expensive-looking, and that when rolled gently between the finger and thumb the tobacco was not dry to the touch. This caused him to give a closer attention to the surface of the carpet than he would otherwise have done. Here again he was rewarded, for in front of an armchair a few inches from its right leg he came upon a little core of cigarette ash. Leaving it where it lay, he moved back the divan to its place against the wall and continued his search. His first concern was to ascertain whether there was a box of cigarettes in the room, or an ash-tray. He made a quick scrutiny of the cupboards and shelves. They had neither one nor the other. The deceased lady, he thought to himself, was no smoker, but this conclusion would have to be verified by the charwoman. He made a mental note of this and continued his search of the floor.

Failing to find anything noteworthy on the other part of the carpet, he continued his search on hands and knees into the little kitchen which opened out of the sitting-room. The light was not very good at this point; the floor of the kitchen was covered with a dark green cork linoleum, and as he crawled forward on his knees his trousers were caught by a nail, happily not so firmly as to tear the cloth. He turned and examined the spot under his reading-glass. He found that the edge of the cork, which had been securely nailed down with flat-headed tacks, had begun to crumble away, leaving one of the tacks to protrude above the surface. Here he made his third discovery. Caught under the head of the tack was a minute shred of dark green wool, of a darker shade even than that of the cork lino. Very gently he detached it from the nail, and opening the back of his watch case he slipped it in and snapped it down again. That was material for another inquiry that must be undertaken the same afternoon. Then he proceeded to make a search of the kitchen itself. It was scrupulously clean and neat, except for a few unwashed articles of crockery lying in the sink—the relics of the dead woman's last meal. On the little kitchen table stood a coffee-pot and boiler combined, and one unwashed coffee-cup. There was an inch deep of cold coffee in the pot and the usual sediment that one finds in a coffee-cup. There was nothing unusual in any of these things, nor did he find anything suspicious in the bathroom beyond. He returned to the sitting-room.

His first care in this room was to open the typewriter, a portable Remington. Without touching the keys or the frame he pulled out of the carrier a half-written letter and read it eagerly.

> "*To all whom it may concern.*
>
> I, Naomi Clynes, have come by easy stages to believe that life is not worth living and that it is no crime to put an end to it. I am sorry for the trouble that I may be causing to a number of worthy people who have been kind to me, but I have neither kith nor kin dependent on me. I have as far as I know no creditors, but in case there are any such you will find in the corner of the drawer in this table a sum of £25 to pay the wages of my charwoman and any other debt that may be justly due. Out of the remainder the simplest possible funeral can be defrayed and the balance paid to Mr. Corder to whom my death may cause trouble."

Richardson now embarked on a proceeding that would have puzzled people who did not know him. He brought his magnifying glass to bear on the spacing bar of the machine and took out from his attaché-case a wide-mouthed bottle of fine white powder. Dipping a camel-hair brush into this, he dusted the powder over the spacing bar and blew off the superfluity. Immediately fingerprints appeared on the black varnish with startling clearness.

Carefully replacing the unfinished letter in the machine, he opened the drawer and examined its contents. Besides the usual adjuncts of the typewriting outfit—rubber, oil-can, paper and carbon, he found £25 in Treasury notes, the sum mentioned in the unfinished letter. These he placed in an official envelope, labelled it and stuck it down. Then he ran downstairs to the milk-shop and asked Mrs. Corder to send Bob, the roundsman, to fetch Annie James, the charwoman, as quickly as possible, and also, if possible, the girl clerk to the Jewish organization on the floor above the flat. Then he returned upstairs to continue his search.

His first discovery on opening the wardrobe was a handbag of black leather. He turned out its contents on the table—a letter in its envelope, £1 17s. 3d. in silver and copper, and a latchkey. He ran downstairs to try it in the lock of No. 37A Seymour Street and found it fitted perfectly. He put it into his pocket for future use.

The letter also he annexed after running over its contents. It was from a firm of publishers—Stanwick & Co.—signed by a member of the firm, with a name he knew—"J. Milsom." It was the last name in the list of the directors embossed on the left-hand corner of the firm's notepaper. The letter was encouraging to a budding authoress. There was nothing in it to hint at professional disappointment.

The rest of the things in the wardrobe consisted of women's clothing, hanging or neatly folded. He felt in every pocket in the garments, but found nothing of any interest. At the back of one of the shelves he came upon a pile of typed manuscript which he packed up to examine at his leisure.

A step sounded on the back stairs—a step which hesitated as it drew near the fatal room. It was Annie James, the charwoman, who stopped with her hand to her mouth when she saw the tall figure of the inspector. "I beg pardon, sir, I'm Miss Clynes' help."

"Oh yes; Annie James is your name, I think."

"That's right, sir."

"Come in. I've really only one question to ask you. Did your late employer smoke?"

"No, sir, that I could swear to. No tobacco ever passed her lips."

"I don't mean to ask whether she was a confirmed and habitual smoker, but you know, Mrs. James, ladies do sometimes indulge in a cigarette. You yourself, for instance."

"Never, sir. For one thing, when my brother gave me one and dared me to smoke it and put a match to it himself, my stomach rose and I was sick. That cured me of smoking for the rest of me life. I remember asking the poor lady once whether she had had the same experience as me, seeing that she didn't smoke, but she told me that she thought it was a dirty habit for women to get into and made the room messy. And that's why you won't find an ash-tray about the place."

"I suppose you gave the room a thorough clean at least once a week."

"Oh, more than that, sir. When I clean a room, I clean it. No dirty corners. 'Clean the corners and the middle takes care of itself': that's what I say."

"And you clean under the bed?" He caught a transient flicker of the eyelids before she replied:

"Yes, sir, I do, regular."

"You had the bed out yesterday morning?"

"Yes, sir, and did it thorough underneath, because the pore lady went out early and I took the opportunity."

"My colleague has told me all you said to him. You haven't forgotten anything else? No? Well then, that's all I think."

Richardson locked the door of the room and slipped the key into his pocket before he let himself out into Seymour Street. He covered the ground to the mortuary at a brisk pace, for he was anxious to find its custodian before the light failed.

The custodian was an old soldier who did not like to have his spell of idleness interrupted.

"It's these police all day long," he muttered, when Richardson tapped on his door. "Well, what is it now?"

Richardson knew how to deal with these municipal Jacks-in-office—knew that it was a waste of time to quarrel with them.

"I'm sorry to trouble you at the end of a busy day," he said pacifically and without any suggestion of irony. "I am Inspector Richardson of the C.I. Department at New Scotland Yard. I want you to let me take the fingerprints and look at the clothing of a woman named Naomi Clynes whose body was brought in this morning."

The man's jaw sank in frank astonishment. "Take her fingerprints, when she's dead? I never heard of such an application before. Take the fingerprints of a living person, that I can understand, but a dead person can't do any more burglaries. So what do you want her fingerprints for?"

"I'm afraid it would take too long to explain, but if you like to come along with me it might interest you to see how it's done."

It was not an easy or an edifying spectacle, for rigor mortis had already set in and Richardson had never had this task thrown upon him before. However, with the help of the custodian, he did succeed in obtaining a set of perfectly legible prints.

"And what are you going to do with these now?" asked the custodian.

"Compare them with some prints that I've found in her room. And now I want you to let me see her outer clothing."

"Right you are, Inspector. Here's the bundle, all rolled up and labelled."

Richardson rapidly untied the bundle and observed that it included a dark green jersey dress. This he spread out on the table under a strong light. He took out his reading-glass and went over the whole surface, dwelling long over a spot in the upper part of the skirt at the back where a shred of wool had been unravelled making what would in time have become a tear. Opening his watch-case he took out the shred that he had found attached to the tack in the doorway of the kitchen. The colour and the substance of the wool matched exactly.

"What becomes of the clothing of deceased persons after the funeral?"

"Well, generally speaking they're handed over to the relatives, and if they don't want them, why they just stay in these racks until we're full up and have to make a clearance."

Richardson strongly suspected that "making a clearance" was a euphemism for a little private transaction with a dealer in old clothes, but he held his peace, merely remarking that this woollen dress would very probably be required to be produced in court and that it must be carefully preserved until the police applied for it.

"Very good," said the man. "You couldn't have it in a safer place than this."

Richardson returned to the flat and packed up his various parcels—the typewriter, the typed manuscript and his attaché-case. He left the flat to walk to the Sloane Square Underground Station quite heavily laden. Before settling down to write his report he had one pressing duty to perform. Instead of entering the main building he ran rapidly up the stairs in Scotland House, which is joined to the main building by what has been termed the "Bridge of Sighs." His destination was the room of Superintendent Willis of the fingerprint department. Being now an inspector he was able to converse with his old patron Willis on more equal terms.

"I've something rather interesting to show you, Mr. Willis," he said, laying the typewriter on the table and removing the cover.

Willis was approaching the date for his retirement, but his interest in the science to which he had devoted so many years of his life was unabated, nor was his keen eyesight beginning to fail.

"What have you got there? When you bring me anything fresh I know that I'm in for trouble, a murder case at least, cross-examination by counsel for the defence, jurymen with eyes dropping out of their heads and possibly a heckling by the judge. You're a bird of ill omen, Richardson."

"I'm sorry for that because I'm feeling rather pleased with myself."

He opened his attaché-case and took out the set of prints taken from the dead woman's finger-tips. "These prints I took from the fingers of a woman who was gassed, or gassed herself, somewhere about midnight last night."

"Nicely taken," said Willis, examining the prints under the light; instinctively he jotted down the formula of classification under each print with a pencil.

"The woman had left this farewell letter on her typewriter."

"H'm," said Willis, "that seems to settle the question of suicide."

"Yes, if she wrote it—but I want you to look at the prints on the spacing-bar."

"Oh, I see, you've been doing a little developing on your own account. They're a bit confused, aren't they, but fortunately the fingers that made these prints were untrained and so they don't all strike at the same point in the bar. It's been a two-finger exercise." (Willis had the bar under his glass.) "Here's one quite detached. It's either the index or the second finger of the right hand, an ulnar loop." He took up the prints of the dead woman and examined those two fingers. He shook his head." Her right index and second finger are both whorls, so the fellow who planted his finger here and wrote that letter was play-acting."

"You say 'fellow.' Couldn't it have been a woman?"

"With claws that size? Never. This print was made by a man—a fairly big man. He's a man of sedentary habits, and the print was made not many hours ago. Look how it has lapped up the powder. The moisture hasn't had time to dry."

"I must get these prints photographed and enlarged to the same scale, unless you'll get it done for me."

"You can leave that to me. You'll have your hands full with the inquest coming on. I suppose that you've some other evidence?"

"Fortunately I have, but not nearly enough yet to outweigh the police surgeon, who is going to swear that it's an ordinary case of suicide by gas-poisoning."

"Then why not call in the great Panjandrum himself? Even the crustiest of coroners bows down before *him*."

"I'll have to see what Mr. Morden thinks about it. I must hurry off if I'm to catch him."

Charles Morden was in his room and alone. "Come in, Mr. Richardson. I suppose that you've not had time yet to find out anything more about that woman in Seymour Street."

"Yes, sir, and before writing my report I want to put you in possession of some new facts. I've reason for believing that it wasn't a suicide at all, but a murder."

Like every officer in the C.I.D., Charles Morden had long ceased to show surprise at the unexpected. "But the police surgeon seems to be satisfied."

"He does, sir, but he made no examination of the woman's organs, and this should, I think, be done by Sir Gerald Whitcombe himself."

"Tell me shortly what you have found."

"In the first place I found this cigarette in the border of the carpet against the bed. The charwoman states that Miss Clynes never smoked and yet I found cigarette ash on the carpet." He took from his pocket an official envelope containing the cigarette and ash. "Secondly, I found, caught in a nail at the entrance to the kitchen, this little piece of wool. I've been to the mortuary to examine the deceased's clothing and I have found that she was wearing a green woollen dress of exactly this shade."

"That doesn't seem conclusive. She might have caught her skirt in the nail days ago."

"Yes, sir, but I've found the place where this shred came from. It was from the back of the skirt and quite high up."

"Could she have fallen in a sitting posture as she went into the kitchen?"

"Certainly, that is possible, sir, but in that case would not she have darned the little rent? There was every evidence that she was careful about her clothes."

"What are you suggesting? That some man was with her in the flat last night and that he dragged her across the floor into the kitchen and pushed her head into the oven? Why, she would have screamed the house down while he was doing it."

"She would, sir, if she was conscious."

"But there were no head injuries."

"No, sir, there were not, but I suppose there are narcotic poisons that might produce unconsciousness. I found a coffee-cup with some dregs in it. This could be analysed."

"Yes, but it might be argued that she swallowed the contents of the cup, turned on the gas, and put her head into the oven."

"Yes, sir, but I found one thing more—a finger-print on the spacing-bar of her typewriter. I've taken her fingerprints and Superintendent Willis has compared them with that print on the bar. He is prepared to swear that the print on the spacing-bar is that of a man. On the machine was this farewell letter."

Morden pursed up his lips as he read it. "Isn't it the kind of letter one would expect that type of woman to write?"

"Possibly, sir, but if you will look at the letter you will see that it is not the work of an expert typist as she was."

Morden scrutinized the letter. "You mean that the force used in striking the keys was uneven?"

"Yes, sir, but not only that: on the fifth line you will notice that one letter is struck over another—a mistake very rarely made by expert typists—and then the fingerprints are not hers."

"H'm! It won't do to spring this on a coroner's jury all at once. Reporters will be round with their tongues hanging out if we do, and that will prejudice your inquiries. At the same time I am against too much bottling-up. I'll have a straight talk to the coroner this evening and try to get him to open the inquest and adjourn it for a week. That will give you breathing space. In the meantime please go on with your inquiry as if nothing had happened."

It is the invariable practice of the Criminal Investigation Department in London, when a complicated criminal case is entrusted to a senior officer, to let him take with him a junior, partly to relieve him of subsidiary inquiries, and partly to serve in corroborating his evidence when given in court.

"You will want to take a sergeant with you," said Morden, with a twinkle, knowing perfectly well on whom Richardson's choice would fall. "I believe that Sergeant Bennett is free at the moment."

"In a case like this, sir, I should like to take Sergeant Williams. I believe that he is free."

"You must settle that with the Chief Constable. Let me know how the case goes on. Your first task ought to be to find the relatives of the dead woman."

Chapter Three

ON THE following morning Richardson, accompanied by Sergeant Williams, unlocked the door of 37A Seymour Street and went upstairs to the flat. They were fitting the key into the door when the head of a fair-haired young woman appeared on the landing above and smiled down at them.

"The people downstairs left a message last night that some gentleman from Scotland Yard wanted to see me, so I came down early on purpose. Are you the gentlemen?"

"Yes; I sent the message to you. Can I come up to your office?"

"Please do, or I'll come down if you like it better."

Richardson was half-way up the stairs before she had finished speaking, and the girl retreated into the bare little office. She was busy with a duster.

"Excuse me, sir. I'm afraid that everything's covered with dust, but you see it's only me that uses the room, and I don't come every day. Now I think that this chair is all right if you'll sit down." She was still unembarrassed and smiling. She turned to dust a second chair for Williams.

Richardson pulled out his notebook. "May I have your name, please?"

"Ellen McDougall, but people generally call me Nellie.'"

"Mine is Inspector Richardson. If you want to see me at any time you've only got to ask for me on the ground floor at New Scotland Yard. I suppose that you've heard the sad news about the lady on the floor below?"

"Yes, and I can tell you that it was an awful shock to me. Whatever could she have done it for?"

"Did you know her well?"

"Not what you'd call well, but we passed the time of day when we met on the stairs, and she used to use the telephone outside on the landing."

"And placed as it is, you could hardly help hearing what she said."

"That's right, but I didn't take any particular notice of what she said."

"Can you remember her asking for any particular name?"

"No, but she always called the same number— Gerrard 6720."

"What did the conversation seem to be about?"

"Perhaps I ought to tell you that one day I overheard her say a funny thing. Of course she didn't know I was listening. Her tone was grave and anxious that morning. She said, 'Oh, you wouldn't stop at murder? I had thought of suicide.' I've been thinking a lot about that conversation since I heard the dreadful news yesterday morning."

Richardson was writing in his notebook. "You are quite sure of the words she used: 'You wouldn't stop at murder. I had thought of suicide'?"

"That's right. Those were her exact words." Richardson looked up at the little face, framed in fair, tousled hair, and saw that it was transfigured with the emotions of the drama. He put a question that brought her back to the dull routine of a workaday life with a bump.

"Who are your employers, Miss McDougall?"

"The Jewish Benevolent Society for the Fulham area."

"Are you the secretary? You'll excuse me saying so, but you don't look a bit like a Jewess."

She laughed. "People are always saying that. I'm no Jewess. I'm from Scotland. You see it's hard for a typist to get a job nowadays, and I just answered an advertisement. I was sent for to be interviewed and the terms were good for what they wanted me to do—make the round of their offices in Fulham and Chelsea, open the letters, lock up any that contained cheques until the next weekly committee meeting, after sending the printed form of receipt and thanks. Most of the letters were applications for help, but members of the committee deal with them personally."

"You have not to do any visiting?"

"No. My only other duty is to attend committee meetings on Thursday evenings and take down the minutes."

"So you haven't very much to do?"

"No, most days there is only half an hour's work. Then I am free. But I have another job to go to in the afternoons. Mr. Aaronson, a member of the committee, has a furniture shop in King's Road, and he employs me to write up his books in the afternoons."

"Can I see a list of your committee?"

"Certainly."

She fumbled in one of the drawers and produced a typed list of names and addresses. Richardson made a copy of it in his notebook.

Ernest Hartmann, 8 Jubilee Road, Fulham (Chairman).
Samuel Weingartner, 27 Queen's Road, Bayswater.
Albert Greener, 31 Lambeth Road.
Amos Harris, 14 Green Street, Fulham.
Henry Aaronson, 103 King's Road, Chelsea.
Peter Stammer, 4 Lower Panton Street, S.W.3.

"What sort of men are they? Are they kind to you?"

"They are all tradespeople, I believe—very respectable men and very polite and kind. If I've any complaint against them it is that I wish they would not all smoke big cigars in this tiny room at committee meetings. I can scarcely get the smell out of the room before the next meeting, and it makes me cough."

"How do they get in?"

"They ring and knock at the door in Seymour Street and I run down and let them in. You see I have the only latchkey."

"And you never let it out of your care?"

"Never—at least..." She hesitated and the colour began to mount in her cheeks, a symptom of embarrassment which was not lost upon Richardson.

"You were saying...?"

"It's Mr. Hartmann's orders that I should never part with the key, but—"

"But you haven't always kept the rule?"

"Between ourselves, Inspector, I did break it once this week, but for goodness' sake don't tell Mr. Hartmann, or I may lose my job."

"You lent the key to somebody?"

"It was only to Mr. Stammer, and he's a member of the committee. He seemed to make such a point of it, and he's a most respectable man. He said that he wanted it for interviewing one of the applicants, and that he would faithfully return it in the morning. I didn't think that there could be any harm."

"Did he return it?"

"Yes, yesterday morning."

"You mean that he had the key in his possession on the night of the suicide in the flat below?"

The girl nodded, but did not speak. Her eyes were dilated with alarm. At last she mastered herself sufficiently to falter, "I hope you won't make a fuss about this, Inspector. I'm sure Mr. Stammer is a most respectable man."

"What is his occupation, do you know?"

"He keeps an antiquity shop at 173 Fulham Road, I've been told."

"Did Mr. Stammer ask you not to tell Mr. Hartmann?"

"Not quite that, but he let me understand that it was a confidential matter between him and me."

"Very well, Miss McDougall, I need scarcely warn you not to part with the key again. Now I'll leave you to get on with your work."

When the two police officers found themselves alone in the flat below they began to converse about what they had heard.

"What do you think about that young woman?" asked Richardson.

"She struck me as being straightforward enough, but I suppose we'll have to put Master Stammer through the hoop."

"We will. The girl was a fool to risk her job by listening to him."

"That telephone conversation she overheard was funny, talking about murder and suicide."

"It was; we'll have to look up that number that the girl gave us and find out who she was talking to. The first thing we've got to do now is to deal with that coffee-cup and see what an analyst will say about it."

From the wardrobe he took a quarto-sized envelope, used, no doubt, by the dead woman for forwarding manuscript, and carried it into the kitchen. The dregs in the coffee-cup on the table and had now dried up. He put the cup into the envelope, labelled it, and stowed it in his pocket.

"Now, Williams," he said; "we'll tackle those house-agents in Lower Sloane Street. You'd better come with me."

It was a bad moment for letting houses and flats; they had the office to themselves. A clerk hurried forward to receive them. "What can I do for you, gentlemen?"

"We want to see your principal, Mr. Harding."

"Very good, sir," said the clerk, leading the way to a door marked private. They found themselves in the presence of a harassed-looking gentleman, sitting at a table, with a ledger before him.

"I must introduce myself, Mr. Harding. I am Inspector Richardson from New Scotland Yard, and this is my colleague, Sergeant Williams. I believe that you had a visit yesterday from Sergeant Hammett of the B Division who called to inquire about the lease of the flat in 37A Seymour Street. The case has now been handed over to me. He tells me that the late Miss Clynes, who took the flat, furnished two references, and I must ask you to allow me to see their replies."

"Very good, sir, I'll have them looked up. Both replies were satisfactory, otherwise we should not have sublet the flat to her." He touched his bell: the clerk appeared. "The Clynes' correspondence," he said.

In less than a minute a thin file was on the table. "Here are the two letters, Inspector; they seem to be all right."

Richardson made a rapid note of their contents. The first was signed Horace Crispin, Vicar, and was dated from St. Andrew's Vicarage, Liverpool, February 23rd. It ran:

"GENTLEMEN,

"I have much pleasure in saying that Miss Naomi Clynes is well and favourably known to me. She is a member of my congregation and a regular communicant, besides being a friend of my wife and a helper in parochial work. I have every reason to think that she would be a satisfactory tenant."

The other letter ran:

"DEAR SIRS,

"Miss Naomi Clynes was in my employment as a clerk for more than ten years. She left me only because I am shortly closing down my business. She was employed in a position of trust, and I believe that she would be a desirable tenant."

The letter was dated from "4 Apsley Terrace, Liverpool," and was signed "John Maze."

Richardson made a shorthand copy of both letters and returned them to Mr. Harding.

"It's a sad business, Inspector, isn't it? I suppose that I mustn't ask you whether you have discovered any reason for her rash act."

"The inquiry is still going on, Mr. Harding," replied Richardson diplomatically.

"Ah! There'll be an inquest, no doubt."

"Yes, an inquest has to be held in all cases of this kind. Good day and thank you."

Richardson had one question to clear up before he interviewed the six members of the Jewish committee who rented the little office over the flat.

He looked at his watch. "Twenty-five minutes past ten. We've plenty of time for another interview before lunch."

"Who are we going to see?"

"Miss Clynes' publishers—Stanwick & Company. Here's their address, 19 Charing Cross Road. Hallo! I never noticed that. They give the very telephone number that Miss McDougall gave us. I shouldn't be surprised to find that J. Milsom, the junior director of Stanwick & Company, is an old acquaintance of mine, who made himself useful in one of Superintendent Foster's cases in Hampstead two years ago. We'll take the Underground to Charing Cross."

The exterior of Stanwick & Co.'s place of business looked as prosperous as painters, gilders and glaziers could make it. A young clerk, sitting before a bookshelf filled with the productions of his firm, was apparently engaged in killing time by perusing a copy of one of the firm's books when he should have been pasting press-cuttings of reviews into the enormous scrap-book lying open on the table before him. At the appearance of Richardson he slipped the book into a drawer and became the busy and assiduous clerk who more than earned his salary. Richardson tendered his card and asked for "Mr. J. Milsom."

The clerk's eyes bulged. The book he had just been reading dealt with a functionary of this metal-Inspector Pilchard—who cut a rather sorry figure in the story when compared with the brilliant young journalist who stood at his elbow and was the real author of the deductions that had made him famous, and here was an inspector in the flesh!

"Mr. Milsom, sir? I'll see whether he's free to receive you."

Left to themselves they scanned the titles of the works in the bookshelves. "The Poisoned Cup"; "A Hidden Hand"; "The Fatal Kris"; "The Mystery of Chinatown"—Messrs. Stanwick & Co. seemed to be making a corner in police mysteries—and Richardson and Williams, having enough mysteries of their own to solve, never read mystery stories when their duties left them time to read anything.

"Mr. Milsom will be very glad to see you, sir, if you'll kindly step this way."

Leaving his sergeant downstairs, Richardson followed his guide to the lift and was shot up to the third floor. The door at the end of the passage was thrown open; his name and rank were chanted by the clerk, and he found himself in a tiny room in which the greater part of the floor-space was occupied by a table piled high with a stack of papers.

"My God!" exclaimed the man, who sprang up from his chair and stretched a welcoming hand across the table, "it is you! So they've moved you up a step! When I read the name on your card I thought it must be another man, and I wondered which of my crimes had at last come to light." He swept a pile of papers from the only vacant chair on to the floor. "Sit down, won't you?"

Richardson squeezed his way round the table and sat down. "I scarcely expected to find that you had become a publisher, sir."

"I'm not surprised at that. It is my uncle's doing. He has a curious prejudice in favour of *work*—hard work—and as I didn't seem to share it, he made one of his lightning journeys from

Montreal to this little village. He chummed up with old Stanwick on the boat, and the old boy poured out all his financial troubles into his sympathetic ear—told him what a hard row a publisher of really *clean* fiction had to hoe, and how, if he couldn't raise a bit of capital, he would have to put up his shutters. 'In these degenerate days,' he said, 'people won't read anything unless there's a seduction or a divorce in it.' My uncle snorted 'You're wrong there. What people want is CRIME, preferably a good, startling murder which could only have been committed by the dean, or possibly one of the canons. Mr. Fidget harnesses his great mind to the job and proves triumphantly that it was the pew-opener. That's what your readers want. I never read any other kind of literature myself—never have—and look what it's done for me!'

"The poor old guy shook his head and looked doubtful. 'See here,' went on my uncle, thinking of me, 'I'll make you a proposition. I've a nephew in England with a very remarkable brain for these things—Scotland Yard calls him in whenever they're really up against it—his name's James Milsom—but he's a singularly modest bloke and doesn't blow his own trumpet on a housetop—he's the very man for you. If you'll form a company and take him on as one of your directors, I'll put ten thousand pounds to add to your capital, but only on the understanding that you'll go hot and strong for detective mysteries. What about it?' Well, money talks, and here I am!"

"Making a success of the business, I hope, sir?"

"Not exactly making our fortunes so far, but we're on the way. Poor dear old Stanwick shudders a bit when I show him one of my dust-covers, but he unfreezes when he looks at our circulation returns. He was shy about frequenting the Athenaeum after taking me into the business, until a bishop stopped him one day in the hall to congratulate him on one of our best sellers. And then someone spoilt it by telling him that the prelate had been preaching against the modern 'thriller,' and had bought some hundreds of them to serve him as a text. But you haven't looked in to gossip about fiction."

"No, sir. I called to ask whether you had heard of the sudden death of a lady you know—Miss Naomi Clynes?"

"Naomi Clynes? Good God! You can't be serious! I wrote to her only two days ago about a book she was publishing with us, and she rang me up next day."

"That must have been only a few hours before her death. Did she seem to be in good spirits?"

"That depends on what you call good spirits. The telephone sounded as if she would have kissed and hugged me if the Postmaster-General had not been listening in. You see, the firm had agreed to publish her first book on a royalty basis, and she put it all down to me. It was a topping yarn."

"Do you happen to know whether she had any private worries?"

"No, I knew nothing about her at all. She shot in the manuscript and I sat down to wade through it, but after reading the first chapter I found that I couldn't lay it down. I couldn't even stop to get my lunch that day. I got one of my co-directors to dip into it, and it hit him in a vital spot, too. What did the poor woman die of? Heart failure?"

"No, sir; she was found with her head in a gas-oven."

"What is it that makes gas-ovens so fatally attractive to Englishwomen? Whenever the landlord calls for the rent, or they are disappointed in love they crawl to the gas-oven, turn on the taps, and set out to meet their Maker. I should have thought that this was a simple case. What did you hope to get from me?"

Richardson's face registered disappointment. "Well, sir, I hoped that you would be able to give me the addresses of her relatives and friends. The coroner has asked us to trace them, and I've been put in charge of the inquiry. So far I don't know anything about her except that she has friends in Liverpool."

"I didn't even know that. When she called here she never talked about herself, but only about her books. She was half-way through a second book for us, and she was so keen about it that when I asked her to come and lunch with me to meet one or two of my friends she refused, saying that she had registered a vow never to accept an invitation until her book was finished. No, Mr. Richardson, if you had asked me for a list of ladies of my acquaintance who would resist the blandishments of a gas-oven, Miss Clynes would have headed it." He stared hard at Richardson. "Ah, I thought so, you don't believe that it was suicide any more than I do. You think that she was knocked out before her head went into that oven. Well, if you want me to butt in and lend you a hand, you know where to find me. I can be useful sometimes, as I think you'll remember in that case of my dear old pal, Poker Moore."

Without directly accepting the offer of help, Richardson took his leave.

From Charing Cross Road to New Scotland Yard is but a step. He signed to his sergeant to follow him into the street, and they stopped for a moment as if to examine the titles of the books exposed in the window.

"James Milsom was the man I knew, but he couldn't help us at all. Before we interview those Jews one of us will have to take a trip to Liverpool, I fancy, but we'll hear what Mr. Morden says about it first. This trip may not help us, but it will appease the coroner."

Charles Morden had a remarkable faculty for laying aside one task and picking up the threads of another. He looked up, and his tired eyes became keenly alert as soon as he recognized his new visitor.

"Well, Mr. Richardson, have you anything fresh to report about that suicide?"

"I have, sir, but I haven't yet had time to write out my report, or to follow up an important clue. I want your authority for running up to Liverpool this afternoon."

"Why to Liverpool?"

"Because the two references Miss Clynes obtained for her lease of her flat both live in Liverpool, and I hope that they will be able to give me information about her friends and relatives."

"Who are they?"

"The clergyman of her parish and a solicitor named John Maze who was her former employer."

"Can't you get the information on the telephone?"

"I might get something, sir, but I want particularly to see them both and get the names and addresses of her friends. One can't well do that on the telephone."

"When would you be back?"

"By to-morrow night or certainly early the next morning, sir. I've still a good deal to do in London. I've seen the clerk belonging to that Jewish Association upstairs, and I find that one of the Board of Directors persuaded her to lend him her latchkey on the night of the alleged suicide. I've brought down with me a coffee-cup with some grounds in it in case you think it advisable to have an analysis made, both of the coffee-cup and the contents of the dead woman's stomach."

"You think that this ought to be done?"

"I do, sir."

"Very well, you can go to Liverpool and get back as soon as you can. Sergeant Williams can take that cup round to be analysed while you're away. If any poison is found we can have a second post-mortem by Sir Gerald Whitcombe."

Chapter Four

MORDEN SAT thinking when he found himself alone. Usually he made up his mind quickly and resumed the work he was doing, but in this case he felt that he was being rushed—rushed by the junior inspector in Central—rushed, probably, into unnecessary expenditure on an expert's fees, and yet—had Richardson ever let the Department down? It would be easy enough to leave things as they were and let a coroner's jury return a verdict of suicide while of unsound mind; nobody would ever be likely to raise the case again; and yet Richardson had always proved to be right hitherto, however fantastic the theory he had put forward might have seemed at the time. He picked up his telephone and asked to be connected with Sir Gerald Whitcombe.

"Is that you, Whitcombe? Look here, I want you to make a P.M. on the body of a woman named Naomi Clynes who was found gassed yesterday morning in 37A Seymour Street, Chelsea. Have you written that down?"

"..."

"The police surgeon of B Division, Dr. Wardell, is certifying that the cause of death was suicide, but one of our men sticks out that it was murder."

"..."

"Yes, that she was given some kind of quick-acting poison and then dragged to the gas-oven while unconscious. I'm sending you up a coffee-cup with dried dregs in it. He suggests that it was used to administer the poison."

"..."

"No, it was just the contrary. All the witnesses so far are agreed that she was in good spirits and had every reason to be so. She was an authoress, and a publisher had just accepted her first book on liberal terms."

"..."

Morden laughed into the telephone. "I agree. In these days it's as good as winning a horse for the Dublin Sweep. Then you'll go right ahead with the P.M. and the analysis? Good." He hung up the receiver.

On reaching Liverpool, Richardson wasted no time. He drove out to St. Andrew's Vicarage and sent in his card. If he had been less hurried he would have reported himself to police headquarters in Dale Street, but that would have entailed a loss of time which he could ill spare.

The vicar himself came to the door with his visitor's card between his fingers. He was a mild-mannered man approaching sixty, one of those clergy who do not seek preferment by self-advertisement, but are content to remain among the hewers of wood and the drawers of water for their church. He invited his visitor into his study and begged him to sit down. Richardson opened his business at once.

"About three months ago, Mr. Crispin, you became a reference to a house-agent in London for a Miss Naomi Clynes."

The poor vicar's face betrayed anxious concern. "Yes, I remember. I do hope that nothing unpleasant has happened."

"The poor lady was found dead in her flat yesterday morning. There is to be an inquest, and the coroner is most anxious to be put into communication with her friends."

"How shocking! My wife will be terribly upset. Miss Clynes was an active member of my congregation—a regular communicant and always ready to help us in the work of the parish. We missed her very much when she left."

"You have known her for some years?"

"Yes, she was in Paris during the Peace Conference, working for some American Society, and when that broke up she came to Liverpool to be near an aunt who has since died."

"Do you know whether she had any other relations?"

"No, I'm sure she hadn't. She told me so herself. It was partly through me that she obtained a post in the office of a well-known solicitor, Mr. John Maze, in this city. Poor thing! She had no money from her aunt, who had only a small annuity which died with her. What do you think was the cause of Miss Clynes' death?"

"The doctor believes that it was a suicide. She was found with her head in a gas-oven."

"Oh, I can scarcely believe that. She was a most level-headed and conscientious church woman. If you would like to see my wife I'm sure she will confirm all I have said."

"I should like to see Mrs. Crispin very much."

The vicar went out to call his wife, a middle-aged lady, who came in fluttering with emotion.

"I simply can't believe it, Mr...."

"Richardson," prompted her husband.

"I simply can't believe it. Miss Clynes was one of the most sensible women I know. She had literary ambitions, and she wrote to me only a few days ago to say that her first novel had been accepted. It was a most cheerful letter; I wish I'd kept it to show you. She was used to living alone, so she wouldn't have got depressed on that account."

"Where did she live?"

"She was in lodgings at 10 Rosewear Road, quite close to the church."

After noting the address Richardson asked, "Had she any intimate friends?"

"No, I believe that I was her greatest friend. She was a reserved woman who did not make friends very easily."

"She never gave you the impression that she had something on her mind?"

The vicar's wife searched her memory. "You know, of course, that she had one great sorrow in her life. She was engaged to an officer in the Liverpool regiment, and he was killed in 1917."

"No, I did not know that, but after seventeen years that could scarcely have been a motive for suicide. Why did she leave Mr. Maze's employment?"

"Only because Mr. Maze was retiring from business. He, poor man, has never been the same since the death of his little nephew. He was taking him to school in France and they were in that dreadful railway accident outside Paris when one train ran over another and half the passengers were killed. He escaped with nothing worse than a shaking, but the boy was killed. Miss Clynes told me that he could not bear to speak of it."

"He spoke of it to me just once," said the vicar.

"He said that the business of identifying the body and arranging for the funeral was the most horrible in his experience."

"Everyone noticed the difference in him," added his wife. "It was natural that he should want to retire. Miss Clynes told me that he had been very generous to her, but of course he could afford it as he is a very rich man."

Richardson slowly closed his notebook, having come to the end of his questions. "Thank you very much. You have been very helpful, Mrs. Crispin. I think that I will call at Miss Clynes' late lodgings and see whether her landlady can throw any light on the cause of her sad death."

The vicar came to the door with him to point out the direction of the lodgings, and they parted with mutual expressions of goodwill.

No. 10 Rosewear Road proved easy to find. The bell was answered by a buxom, smiling landlady, who wilted a little when she heard who he was, but invited him into her kitchen in order not to disturb her lodgers who were at supper in the parlour.

"I have called to ask you a few questions about the late Miss Clynes, who, I am told, formerly lodged with you."

"The *late* Miss Clynes, sir? Do you mean that she's dead? How dreadful! It must have been very sudden."

"It was. There is to be an inquest, because she was found dead yesterday morning with her head in the gas-oven."

"Never! She wasn't one to commit suicide. She lodged with me for years, and if she'd had any troubles I'm sure she'd have told me. Not that she was one to talk about herself, but she was always one to look on the bright side, and only a week or two ago she wrote me such a nice bright letter to say that all was going well with her writing and she was very happy in London. Dear, dear! One never knows. 'In the midst of life we are in death,' as Shakespeare used to say."

"Had she any friends—people who came to tea with her, for instance—while she was lodging with you?"

"I can't say that she had any special friend. There was, of course, Mrs. Crispin from the Vicarage, and some of the other ladies who do Church work, and sometimes one or other of them would stay to tea, but when I say no special friend, there was none of them that she called by their Christian name."

"Have you kept the letter she wrote to you from London?"

"No, sir, I'm afraid I haven't. The few letters I get have to be used for lighting the fire."

"Apparently she wasn't a lady who made friends very easily. Did she make enemies?"

"Good gracious! No! She was the quietest, gentlest woman that you'd meet anywhere, and yet she could hold her own when it came to the point. Why, one morning, from my kitchen window, I saw her out in the road without a hat, trouncing a boy who'd set his dog at a poor little kitten. He didn't get away from her without hearing some home truths, I can tell you."

"When she decided to go up to London did she seem pleased to be leaving Liverpool?"

"I think she was looking forward to it on the whole, sir. You see, it was a new adventure, but sometimes she'd get thoughtful like, as if she was wondering how she'd get on up there."

"Thank you, Mrs. Clark. I think that that's all I need ask you."

"Good-bye, sir. I shall watch the papers for that inquest."

The church clock was striking eight as Richardson left Rosewear Road: it was not too late for his visit to John Maze at his private address, which was in the residential part of Liverpool. The butler who opened the door to him exhibited surprise at receiving a visitor at such an hour, and even greater surprise when he read the name on the card which was tendered to him. "Is Mr. Maze expecting you, sir?"

"Probably not. I should not have dreamed of disturbing him at such an hour if the matter were not urgent. Will you tell him that I shall not detain him for more than a few minutes?"

He was shown into the library—a room furnished luxuriously with dark leather armchairs and a carpet into which the feet sank deep. He was not kept waiting. A tall man in a dinner-jacket opened the door. He was past middle age, but he was still erect and active in his movements. He held Richardson's card in his hand.

"Good evening, Inspector. I'm very glad to see you. Sit down and tell me what I can do for you." He took the armchair opposite to Richardson. "Perhaps before we discuss business we had better wait until we know that we shan't be disturbed. They are bringing us a glass of port."

The door opened and the butler brought in a tray carrying a decanter, glasses and biscuits, which he set down between them. As soon as they were alone Richardson spoke.

"The Assistant Commissioner sent me to see you, sir, on the subject of a reference you signed for a Miss Naomi Clynes when she engaged her flat in Chelsea."

"I remember perfectly. Why, has anything gone wrong?"

"She's dead, sir."

"Good God! Her death must have been very sudden. What was the cause of it?"

"It is ascribed to suicide. She was found in the morning lying in her kitchen with her head in the gas-oven with all the taps turned on. There is to be an inquest, of course, and the coroner has applied to the police for information about her relatives and friends. She seems to have had no friends in London, and that is why I am making inquiries in Liverpool."

"The news is a great shock to me. She was my confidential clerk and worked for me for ten years until three months ago, and if I had searched the country through I should never have found a better one. I'm afraid, poor woman, that she can't have made a success of her new venture."

"According to her publishers, things were going well. Do you happen to know anything of her life before she came to Liverpool?"

"She told me that she had been working for one of those American philanthropic societies that were formed in Paris at the time of the Peace Conference, and they gave her the highest character. At first she was living with an aunt in Liverpool, but three or four years later the aunt died and she told me that she was the last relation she had in the world. She was a curiously reticent creature; even her fellow-clerks seem to have known very little about her."

"May I ask why she left her employment with you?"

"Only because I am retiring from business and have no longer any need of a secretary. I wanted to do my best for her, as one always does for a faithful employee who has been with one for years. Quite by chance I had heard from one of the other clerks that in her spare time Miss Clynes had been writing for one of the magazines and had had a story accepted, and that she had literary ambitions. I made a jocular allusion to this, and she told me quite seriously that it was true; that her dream was to establish herself in London and devote herself seriously to writing. This seemed to be an opportunity for helping her. I broke the news to her that I was going to close down the office, but that I would give her twelve months' salary in lieu of notice and let her go at once if she liked, and that, of course, she could give my name as a reference in case she found another employer. She seemed very grateful and she wrote to me from London, asking me to become her reference for a little flat she was taking. I suppose, poor woman, that she must have found the market for fiction as overcrowded as everything else in these days, and that this depressed her..."

"No, sir, on the contrary, she had just had her first novel accepted on very favourable terms."

"Indeed? That surprises me very much. I shouldn't have thought that she was a woman of imagination, though the English she used in my correspondence was very good. A first novel! On good terms, too! It's surprising, and it makes her suicide all the more astonishing. She wasn't the kind of woman to have an unfortunate love-affair."

"Have you seen her at all since she went to London, sir?"

"No, and I fear that I haven't kept the one letter of thanks she wrote to me."

Richardson finished his glass of port and rose to take leave. "I am very much obliged to you, sir, for receiving me at such an untimely hour. It will enable me to get away to London by an earlier train than I thought possible."

"You said that there was to be an inquest, Inspector. I suppose that that will throw some light on the mystery. The doctors are satisfied about the cause of death, no doubt?"

"So I understand, sir. The case is sure to be reported in the London papers. Good night, sir."

Having the invaluable faculty of being able to sleep in the train, Richardson arrived at headquarters feeling quite fresh and ready for work. It was rather early for finding the Assistant Commissioner in his office: he sought out his Chief's messenger and asked him to report that he had returned from Liverpool.

"You can do that yourself, Inspector; Mr. Morden came early this morning."

"Then will you ask him if he can see me?"

"You haven't been long, Mr. Richardson," said Charles Morden. "I counted on your being away for the whole of to-day."

"I was lucky, sir. I found all the people I had to see at home yesterday evening."

"What did they say?"

"All confirmed what we had heard. The vicar and his wife seemed to have known Miss Clynes better than the others. They both scouted the idea that she could have committed suicide, though it appears that she had a great sorrow during the war, but that was seventeen years ago. Then I went to see her landlady, but I got nothing out of her except that she had had a letter from Miss Clynes written in good spirits. My last interview was with Mr. John Maze who had given her a reference for the house-agents. I had been told by the vicar's wife that she had left his service because he was retiring from business. He confirmed this when I saw him, and told me that as a recognition of her work he had given her a year's salary in lieu of notice."

"What was Maze like?"

"A man past middle age, sir, living in solid comfort in a big house. He was a solicitor, but he has lately retired and is believed to be a rich man. All four of these people seemed ready to tell me everything they knew: all four had received letters from Miss Clynes, but none of them had kept her letters. The only relative that the dead woman had in the world seems to have been an aunt who died two or three years ago."

"So practically you had your journey to Liverpool for nothing."

"Not quite that, sir. We have confirmation of the statement that the dead woman had everything to make her content with life, and nothing to induce her to kill herself."

"Well, I have more news for you than you have for me. Sir Gerald Whitcombe rang me up this morning to say that last night he made an analysis of the contents of that coffee-cup and found traces of aconitina in it."

"A poison, sir?"

"Yes. Aconitina, he said, is the alkaloid of aconite, and one grain of it is enough to cause death. One of the first things you had better do is to make a thorough search of her flat for any bottle or packet that may have contained the beastly stuff."

"Very good, sir, I will. I suppose it's a scheduled poison?"

"Oh, yes. She couldn't have obtained it easily from any chemist. But you mustn't run away with the idea that it proves your case: she may very well have taken the drug herself and then gassed herself to make sure of the job. Don't waste any time in writing up your report; you have plenty to do to-day. Sir Gerald is conducting his post-mortem at this moment."

"Very good, sir; I'll go down to the flat at once."

Richardson looked in at the detective sergeant's room where he found Williams busy writing up his notes.

"Back already, Inspector?" he said. "We didn't expect you until to-morrow morning. Things have been warming up here."

"So Mr. Morden tells me. You'd better lock up those notes of yours and come down with me to the flat. We've got a job of work to do."

They looked in at the milk-shop to inquire whether there had been any development during the past twenty-four hours.

"Yes, sir, there has been. Bob, our roundsman, has something to tell you. He's out at the back washing his cans: I'll call him."

The roundsman made his appearance sheepishly as he rolled down his shirt-sleeves.

"Bob, I want you to tell this gentleman what you told us last night—about what you saw in Seymour Street that night."

"It wasn't very much, sir. You see I'd been over to the Grape Vine for my usual glass of beer, and I was passing across the end of Seymour Street on my way back when I saw a fellow just disappearing into the door of 37A."

"What time was that?"

"I always go the same time. It must have been a few minutes after half-past eight."

"It's dark then. Would you be able to recognize the man if you saw him?"

"I couldn't swear to him, but I saw him plain in the street light. He went in and shut the door behind him without making a sound."

"Did you see only his back view?"

"No, I saw him sideways."

"What did he look like?"

"Well, he was shortish and he had a hooky nose. I took him for one of them Jews that have that office upstairs, but it seemed funny to me to see him coming to the office at that hour, and then he seemed to be sneaking in as if he didn't want to be seen."

"Thank you, Robert, I'm glad you told me that."

When they were in the flat with the door shut, Richardson stood for a moment thinking. "We've got our hands full, Williams, and it's difficult to know what to get on with first. The Chief wants the flat searched for a bottle or a packet of poison; we've got to see the coroner about those witnesses from Liverpool, and then there's the question of that man the roundsman saw sneaking into Seymour Street that night. As we're here we'd better begin with the searching and take our coats off to it."

Williams smiled meditatively while slipping off his coat and turning up his shirt-sleeves. "What that young woman, McDougall, told us about the key, coupled with what Bob the roundsman saw—a Jew-boy sneaking in through the door—is beginning to make me form a theory about this case."

"That's where you're wrong, Sergeant Williams. Never start forming theories at the beginning of a case or you'll find that they'll let you down."

Chapter Five

RICHARDSON had reduced the searching of rooms to a fine art. His proceedings were punctuated with a running commentary intended to smooth the way for his subordinate.

"We're looking for bottles first and for paper packets second. Bottles and powders are generally kept in the bathroom. Come along, Williams, and tackle the medicine-cupboard."

Williams cleared the cupboard of its contents, ranging them on the tiny table. "The bottles are nearly all empty, Inspector. Here's one paper packet marked 'Camphorated chalk' and it smells of camphor."

"You'd better pack them all in that attaché-case whether they're empty or not. Now for the wardrobe in the next room. There's one thing worth remembering. When people want to hide letters or thin paper packets, they put them either under the carpet or they turn a drawer upside down and fasten the thing to the bottom with a drawing-pin, so a search is never complete until you've examined the underside of each drawer."

Williams went to work methodically and exhibited the bottoms of the drawers guiltless of any sinister concealments, but he treasured the hint for use in the future.

The top shelf was too high for any but a very tall woman to reach without a chair. At the extreme back of it Richardson found a small leather jewel-case locked, but one of the keys in the dead woman's handbag fitted it. He spread out its contents on the table. There were three or four pieces of jewellery in ancient settings—probably heirlooms, for they were too clumsy to be worn in these days. At the bottom of the jewel-case he came upon part of a torn envelope bearing a French postage stamp for one franc fifty and a postmark.

Richardson pulled out a reading-glass and scrutinized it. "Here, Williams, your eyes may be quicker than mine. See what you can make of the postmark."

"It's pretty faint, but it's a place with a double name, and the stamp is French 'C-L-E-R—' I can't make out the next two letters, but N-T are clear enough. Then the next word starts with an F. 'F-E-R-R—'"

"Isn't there a place right in the middle of France called Clermont-Ferrand? See how that fits the letters."

"By Jove! I believe you've hit it. Yes—Clermont-Ferrand it is."

"Now, Williams, set that brain of yours to work. Why should that poor woman have kept that postage-stamp among her jewellery? She wasn't a stamp-collector."

"Sentiment, I should think. Perhaps her young man who was killed in the war wrote to her from there."

"Go to the bottom of the class. You haven't looked at the date, man, 13-2-34. That means that someone wrote to her from Clermont-Ferrand three months ago. What do you make of that?"

Sergeant Williams scratched his chin in deep thought. "I give it up, Inspector."

"You must never give things up, least of all the trifles you come across in a case like this. On this postage-stamp may hang the solution of this murder. After all, smaller things than this have brought men to the gallows. Give me one of those official envelopes and I'll seal up this stamp in your presence."

The stamp, having been duly sealed up and labelled, Richardson slipped on his coat.

"Have we finished here?" asked Williams.

"Yes; I went over the floor thoroughly the first day. I don't think that I left a square inch of it unsearched."

"Where are we going next?"

"To interview Mr. Peter Stammer, the Hebrew gentleman who keeps a curiosity shop at 173 Fulham Road. We'll put him through the hoop."

"Yes, and I fancy that you'll come upon something a bit more promising than a postage-stamp."

"We may, or we may not. At any rate we shall have some fun with him."

The shop front at No. 173 Fulham Road proved to be artistically arranged. True, the antiquities exposed in the shop window were not priced, but in all other respects they were attractive enough to catch the unwary. The shop door rang an electric bell which continued ringing until the door was shut. Out of the gloom of the back shop emerged an oily-looking young Hebrew like a spider from the corner of its web.

"What can I do for you, gentlemen?" he inquired, washing his hands in invisible soap.

"Am I speaking to Mr. Peter Stammer?"

"That is my name, sir," replied the gentleman, after some hesitation.

"I am Inspector Richardson from New Scotland Yard." Richardson knew how to open hostilities with this type of tradesman, and saw with satisfaction that the shot had told.

"Yes, sir?"

"You were in the office at the top of 37A Seymour Street on Tuesday night."

"No, sir, you are mistaken."

"I think not. You borrowed the latchkey from Miss McDougall, the clerk of your committee. I learned that from questioning her. She did not volunteer the information."

"Yes, sir, that's quite true, but I didn't use it. Didn't she tell you that too?"

"No, she did not. Come, Mr. Stammer, you'd better own up. You went up to the office a few minutes after half-past eight that evening."

"If anyone says that he saw me he's a liar, and I'll tell him that to his face."

"I suppose that you've heard that a woman was found dead next morning in the flat below your office."

The man became livid with fear, but he made a brave attempt to bluster. "So that's what it is! You detectives aren't equal to finding out who was responsible, so you're going to try and fix it on me! If that's your game you'll find out your mistake. I can apply to the courts for protection, and get it, too."

"Your best method to get protection, as you call it, is to tell the truth about your visit to the house at night, and what you went there for. You know very well that you had no right to borrow that key. When your chairman comes to know about it, he'll have something to say."

"I tell you I never used the key," he said doggedly.

"Very well, Mr. Stammer. If you think better of your denial you know where to find me. Good day."

When they were clear of the shop Williams remarked, "I hoped you were going to press him further, Inspector. He was getting frightened."

"I know he was, but I would always rather have a voluntary admission than a confession wrung from a man by fear."

"But do you think that he'll make a voluntary admission?"

"I rather fancy that he will before we've done with him. I'm going to try the method of open observation this evening, but he's seen you, and I'd like him to find a new face on the job. I'm going to call in Sergeant Hills for a few minutes this evening. Mean-while we've got the other members of the committee to see. We'll tackle the chairman first."

Ernest Hartmann, the chairman of the Jewish committee, lived at 8 Jubilee Road, Fulham. It proved to be a furniture shop, and they found its proprietor in a little glazed office at the back of the shop. He was a very different kind of man from the blustering Stammer—an old man with a grey beard and a kindly look in his eyes which inspired confidence.

"Can I have a word with you in private, Mr. Hartmann? I am Inspector Richardson from New Scotland Yard. Here is my card."

"Certainly, sir. We shall be quieter in the back shop, I think. I'll show you the way."

He led them into a store-room for spare furniture, pulled out three chairs and dusted them, inviting his visitors to sit down.

"You are chairman of a philanthropic society with an office in 37A Seymour Street, I am told."

"Yes, sir, I was the founder of the committee and am now its chairman and treasurer."

"What are its objects, may I ask?"

"To help the poorest of our co-religionists in this part of London. We collect funds from the more wealthy Jews and distribute them in the form of help in kind, not money, because to give them money is like trying to fill a bucket with a hole in it. I started the work single-handed, but I soon found that it was too much for one man, and I formed a committee, sending the names to the subscribers for approval. We do not interview applicants for relief in our office, but each member of the committee makes himself responsible for visiting a certain number of the cases in their homes, and, in deserving cases, helping them."

"No doubt you have heard of the tragedy in the flat below your office on Tuesday night."

"No, sir. I haven't been to the office these last few days. What was it?"

"The occupant of the flat below your office was found gassed."

"You don't say so. Was it an accidental death?"

"No. The doctor who examined the body thinks that it was a suicide. There is to be an inquest."

"I passed that lady on the stairs once. She seemed very cheerful and polite."

"So everybody says. I have seen Miss McDougall, your secretary, and she can throw no light on the matter. I understand from her that she is the only person entrusted with a latchkey."

"Yes, and she has strict orders not to lend it to anybody— not even to a member of the committee. I do not think that she would dare to disobey that rule."

"My reason for asking is that it has been suggested that the dead woman had a visitor that evening, and I thought it possible that someone might have gained access to your office and hidden himself there. I understand that the door of your office is not kept locked."

"That is because occasionally a charwoman comes in to clean it, and there is no fixed hour for this. But I can't think that anybody could have got in."

"Every member of your committee knows, I suppose, that he must not ask your secretary for the loan of her key?"

"Yes, every member. If I knew that the rule had been broken it would go hardly with the member and the secretary. Is it suggested that it was a murder and not a suicide?"

"We shall know that after the inquest, Mr. Hartmann. The doctors will give evidence of the cause of death. The case is an interesting one, and the verdict of the jury is sure to be published in the Press. Now I must take up no more of your time."

"One thing before you go, sir. You seemed just now to think it possible that the rule about that latch-key might have been broken. If you find any evidence that it was, I hope that you will not fail to let me know."

"Certainly, if I get the permission of my chiefs to do so."

There was nothing new to be learned from the other members of the committee. All four were elderly Jewish shopkeepers with unblemished records, and had been engaged in charitable work among their poorer co-religionists for several years.

At the end of the last interview Richardson told Williams to return to the Central Office and write a precis of the statements made to them by members of the Jewish Committee. He himself sought out Sergeant Hills, a colleague whose home lay in Fulham, and made him a proposal.

"It's a fine evening, George. Why shouldn't you walk home with me?"

"What are you getting at? You don't live in my direction."

"No, I don't, but I want you to help me in a little job of observation. We can start as soon as you like."

"Young man, if you think that I'm going to give up any of my free time to keep observation in one of your cases..."

"It's not an ordinary case of observation, and it won't take you more than ten minutes."

"A funny kind of observation!"

"Yes, it doesn't follow any of the rules we learned in the class. It is what I call open observation. You know that Jew-boy's curiosity shop at No. 173 Fulham Road? You must have passed it every morning ever since you married."

"I've passed it, but I've never been into it."

"Well, I want to give the owner a turn. He's a persistent kind of liar, and he's inclined to be uppish, but when he sees two detectives posted outside his shop when he pulls down the shutters, and one of them following him home, he'll pass a sleepless night and come running down here to see me to-morrow morning—that is, if he's the kind of worm I take him for."

"All right, I'll come, but remember I'm booked to take my missus and kiddy to the pictures this evening, and if I'm late I shall get it in the neck. We'd better start right away."

Lest it be thought that in their free hours men of the C.I.D discuss their cases with one another, or read detective fiction, let me hasten to assure the reader that they leave the cares of office behind them when they go off duty, and that their nearest approach to violence is watching a boxing-contest between police officers of the A Division. As these two walked westward at a brisk pace, Hills asked his companion whether he went to the pictures.

"No," said Richardson, "when I go to shows at all I like the stage, and you see one gets a few complimentaries during the year."

"I used to be like you," said his companion; "I'd no use for the pictures, but it's different when one's married. My missus is wild about them, and gradually she's roped me in."

"Certainly there's this about the pictures—that they can show you things that you can never see on the stage."

They were nearing their destination. Richardson was looking at his watch, for he wanted, if possible, to hit off the moment when Peter Stammer would be putting up the shutters of his shop. It was a little soon for that; his attention would have to be attracted to the street by some other means.

"You stand here, George, well forward to the kerbstone, and stare at the shop while I cross the road and do a little peering."

He dodged behind an omnibus, and after pausing for a few moments in front of the shop window, he approached the door, stooped and peered in. He could see no sign of life, but he crossed the road to his friend and asked him to watch any movement behind the plate-glass window while he strolled up and down the pavement in full view of the shop. Hills recalled him with a peculiar whistle which he knew.

"Your Jew-boy is on the move; he's watching us with his eyes on stalks, like a prawn's. He looks as if he was scared stiff. Oh, here he comes."

Mr. Peter Stammer came out of his shop with a brave show of indifference. He carried out the shutters and lifted them into their places and, having locked up his shop, emerged boldly with his nose in the air and set out at a brisk pace.

"Thank you, old man. Good night. I'll have to step out or I shall lose him."

The corner of a side street gave the fugitive Stammer an opportunity of glancing behind him to see whether he was being followed. The glance was not reassuring. His figure as he resumed his walk was furtive: he had become the hunted quarry. He walked so fast that Richardson was quite glad when he boarded an omnibus that had just pulled up to set a passenger down. It was away before Richardson could reach it, but that, too, was a relief, for now he felt sure that the charm would work. It is a depressing experience for anyone to know that he is being followed.

When Richardson got back to the Central Office to gather up some papers to take home with him, he learned from a messenger that a conference was in progress in Charles Morden's room.

"Did Mr. Morden ask you where I was to be found? The conference may have to do with that case of mine."

"He said nothing about you, Inspector. If you want to go off duty, in your place I should go. They've only just started their conference, and if you wait you may be here half the evening."

"Who are *they*?"

"Well, there's Sir Gerald Whitcombe, the Home Office pathologist; there's the coroner, and Mr. Morden himself."

"Oh, very well, then I'll be off."

In Charles Morden's room Sir Gerald Whitcombe was speaking. "I would much prefer to know that only formal evidence were taken to-morrow, and the inquest adjourned for a week."

"Without calling any medical evidence at all, Sir Gerald?" asked the coroner.

"Oh, no; I should take Dr. Wardell's evidence. Of course he was with me throughout the post-mortem and is in full agreement with me that there was not one cause of death, but two, either of which would have proved fatal. In default of other evidence it might be held that the woman drank the aconitina out of the coffee-cup found in the kitchen, and then put her head into the gas-oven to make sure of the job. That, no doubt, would be the line of defence in a murder trial, and no purely medical evidence could refute it. In cross-examination both Dr. Wardell and I would have to admit it. All that Dr. Wardell would say would be that he was present when the body was found, and that its appearance was consistent with gas-poisoning. In adjourning the inquest you could tell your jury that it is taking time to find the friends of the dead woman and to obtain the results of the post-mortem examination, and that in your opinion it would be premature to find a verdict before all the available evidence was put before them. What do you say, Mr. Morden?"

"I should prefer an adjournment too. Let me put all my cards on the table, Mr. Coroner, and you shall judge for yourself. We have definite evidence that the dead woman was not alone in the flat that night. A typed but unsigned letter headed, 'To all whom it may concern' was found in her typewriter. It declared her intention to commit suicide, but in the opinion of people who can speak with authority, it was not written by a skilled typist as her typing shows her to have been, but by an unskilled amateur. This view is further borne out by a fingerprint found on the spacing-bar of the machine, which is not the print of any of her fingers."

"But if she used the machine, surely there must have been marks made by her fingers on the spacing-bar," objected the coroner.

"You know what these professional typists are, especially when the machine is their own property. They treat it like a sick child; wipe and dust every flat surface in it before they put it away. Then there is evidence that she never smoked, and yet a cigarette of an expensive make was found on the floor together with traces of cigarette-ash on the carpet. There was no ash-tray in the room."

"Shall I have evidence of all this?"

"You will, and when the inquiry is complete I believe that you will have a good deal more. One of our best men is carrying out the inquiry, but I won't undertake that in the next eight days he will have sufficient evidence to enable your jury to find a verdict of murder against any particular person. All that we want now is to give him time without having a crowd of reporters waylaying him whenever he goes out. A mystery of this kind will set Fleet Street humming, whereas none of them will worry about what appears to be an ordinary suicide of a lonely woman."

"Very well," said the coroner; "I will do as you say—take formal evidence at the inquest and adjourn it for a week."

Chapter Six

IT WAS nearly eleven o'clock next morning when the messenger looked into the room that Richardson shared with other inspectors to say that a young man was in the waiting-room to see him.

"A young man with a hooked nose?"

"Yes; he says that he wants to see you in private."

"Very well; tell him to sit tight in the waiting-room: I'll come."

It was a very different Peter Stammer that Richardson found in the waiting-room—a Peter Stammer whose sin had found him out. The inspector regarded him gravely. "You've been wise in coming to me, Mr. Stammer; otherwise the blow might have fallen. Now, before you begin to tell me the truth let me warn you that it must be the whole truth and nothing but the truth, and that if you keep anything back from me you will be making things worse for yourself than they were before. You've come to tell me that you did use the key that night."

"Yes, sir, I did."

"And that you did enter 37A Seymour Street a little after half-past eight."

"Yes, sir."

"Why did you go there?"

"I'd rather not tell you that, sir; it would be compromising another person."

"Oh, of course, I knew that, but you are not going to tell me a fairy story about her being an applicant for relief. It was a girl, wasn't it?"

"Yes, sir, but I hope you won't tell Mr. Hartmann."

"I shan't if I'm satisfied that you are going to tell me the whole truth. How long were you upstairs with that girl?"

"I can't tell you exactly, sir, but I know I was home very soon after ten."

"So you were about two hours in the office upstairs, and I suppose that you crept up very quietly, both of you."

"Yes, sir."

"Did you hear any voices or any sounds at all in the flat below as you passed the door?"

"Not as we went up, sir, but when we came down just after ten I heard people talking in low voices; one of them was a man's voice."

"Did they appear to be disputing?"

"No, sir; it seemed like a friendly conversation. Of course, I never stopped to listen; I was too much afraid that Miss Clynes' visitor, whoever he might be, would come out and catch us."

"So that's all you can tell me."

"Yes, sir; I've told you everything I know, and now I do hope that you'll say nothing to Mr. Hartmann about that key."

"I shall say nothing unless it becomes necessary in the interests of justice to call you as a witness, but as a matter of form you'll have to give me the name and address of the young woman who was with you."

"Must I, sir?"

"Certainly you must."

Peter Stammer heaved a sigh; the net of embarrassment had closed round him: there was no escape.

"Miss Rose Cohen, 93 Lambeth Road."

"Her occupation?"

"Shop assistant, sir, but I do hope that the name won't come out; it would kill the poor girl if it did."

"Now, Mr. Stammer, I must get this down on paper and ask you to sign it before you go. Just sit here; I shan't be long." And to the messenger as he passed him he said, "Just keep an eye on him and see that he doesn't leave the building."

He wrote out the statement rapidly and returned to the waiting-room. "Kindly sign here, Mr. Stammer. As I told you, if I find that you've told me the whole truth I shall try to keep you out of the case, and if you feel like taking my advice never attempt to borrow that key again."

"No, sir, you can rely upon it that I won't."

Richardson smiled as he thought of Sergeant Williams' disappointment when he came to hear of the tame ending to the adventure on which he had been building his theory. He spent the rest of the morning in making his final examination of the dead woman's papers. He did not, of course, wade through every page of the half-finished novel which she had typed, but he scrutinized every other scrap of paper that he had found in her cupboard.

"There's a gentleman to see you, Inspector," announced the messenger. "Name of Milsom."

"Have you put him in the waiting-room? Tell him I'll come."

Jim Milsom rose and shook hands with cordiality. "I've come straight from the inquest on that poor lady. Lord! What a slow country this is! The whole thing was over in less than fifteen minutes."

"Then why do you call it a slow country, Mr. Milsom?"

"Because there wasn't a man in that dreary little court-house who said anything that we didn't know before. It was a pure waste of public time. The coroner rapped out his piece as if he'd learnt it by heart—the doctor the same. Then the coroner adjourned the proceedings for a week. I was the public; there was no one else—not a solitary reporter to write up the proceedings; it was a real dishonour to that poor lady's memory. Why, on the other side of the water we put some zip into it. If the police can't find a murderer, why the reporters do it for them."

"Reporters are apt to be a nuisance to the police, Mr. Milsom."

"You wouldn't mind them if they boosted you as the greatest criminologist of the century and called you a 'well-tailored dude, the highly-skilled sleuth of the homicide squad.' Think what an inspiration and encouragement that would be."

"I'm getting on quite nicely without that."

"You are; that's what I came round to ask you—that and leave to read the manuscript of Miss Clynes' unfinished story. It'll have a high publicity value when we've discovered the murderer. I suppose that you're convinced now that it was a murder. Have you found anyone belonging to her yet?"

"No near relative, I'm sorry to say, but one or two friends and acquaintances in Liverpool."

"But surely there must have been addresses in that diary of hers. She was always pulling it out and making notes in it when I talked to her."

"There was no diary among her papers, Mr. Milsom."

"The devil there wasn't! Then someone must have pinched it."

"There were no private papers at all, except a letter from you which I found among these pages and her bank pass book. There was not even a cheque book."

"You're getting warm, Richardson. The man who did her in must have pinched all her private papers, and I'll be shot if I understand why. Well, I must be trotting along. I suppose I can't tempt you out to lunch? You could meet a fair lady novelist with horned spectacles and a squint who'll make your flesh creep if she lets herself go: she's our latest big noise in the thriller world."

"Thank you very much, Mr. Milsom, but I can't accept your invitation to-day: I've too much to do."

Morden's messenger had promised to tell Richardson when his Chief returned from lunch and to arrange for an interview with him. He made his appearance at half-past two.

"Mr. Morden will see you now, Inspector."

"Good; I'll come."

"Well, Mr. Richardson, the inquest has been adjourned for a week: that will give you time to get on with your inquiry. You know, of course, that Sir Gerald found traces of poison in that coffee-cup and since then he found traces in the body itself. So far there is nothing inconsistent with your theory. You think that a man was in the flat that evening; that he contrived to drop poison into the woman's coffee-cup and that when the poison had begun to act he dragged her into the kitchen on her back and pushed her head into the oven."

"Yes, sir, and I think that he then came out of the kitchen, typed that letter and made a hurried search for her diary and all her private correspondence. He couldn't stop to go through them because of the gas, so he took them all away to search for the letter he had written to her making the appointment. I know from the milk-woman downstairs that she received a letter that morning. The postman gave it to her instead of taking it round to the flat because she was just going up with the milk. I haven't been able to find that letter anywhere in her flat."

"No; but some people make a habit of destroying their letters as soon as they've read them."

"Quite so, sir. But the milk-woman always took up her weekly bill on Tuesday morning, and she did so on the morning of Miss Clynes' death. She states that Miss Clynes made a point of looking in on the following day to pay it and to get it receipted. I didn't find that bill, sir. Her publisher has just told me that she kept a diary in which she entered everything; that he has seen the diary himself; yet it was not in her flat when I searched it."

"Did you search the pockets of her clothing and her handbag?"

"Yes, sir—Sergeant Williams and I searched thoroughly. There was nothing in any of the pockets, but one thing I did find. This French stamp and postmark torn off an envelope. It was hidden right at the bottom of her little leather jewel-case."

Morden examined the stamp. "'Clermont-Ferrand, February 13th, 1934.' Why, that is only a short time before she took over the flat. I wonder why she kept it so carefully. You mustn't lose this, Mr. Richardson."

"No, sir; you'll find it with my report. But I ought to tell you that there is further evidence that a man was in her flat that evening."

"Oh, that's new. How do you know?"

"One of the Jewish committee upstairs had borrowed the latchkey from the secretary that evening. As it was strictly against the rules of the committee, at first he denied that he used the key, but he's been here to-day to admit that he told a lie; that he was there with a girl whose name and address he gave me, and that when passing the door of the flat on their way out he overheard conversation in a male and female voice."

"What time was that?"

"A few minutes after ten, sir."

"Do you think he was telling the truth?"

"Yes, sir, I believe that he was. I've taken his statement. I've also fetched away from the flat all the medicine bottles I could find, but there were no paper packets or pill-boxes bearing a chemist's name. With your permission, sir, I will take the bottles round to Sir Gerald."

"Yes, please do so. Sir Gerald may find some trace of poison in one of the bottles."

"In view of the care with which Miss Clynes preserved that postage-stamp, would it not be wise to write to Mr. John Maze in Liverpool and ask him if he has still kept the references given by that American society in Paris for Miss Clynes when she entered his employment?"

"You mean that that would give us the address of these people and enable us to trace some friend of Miss Clynes who may still be living in France?"

"Yes, sir."

"Very well, ask Superintendent Cox to draft a letter for my signature. Give him all the necessary particulars."

And then one of those strokes of luck which lighten the labours of all detectives in the course of their career befell Inspector Richardson. On the way back to his room the messenger waylaid him.

"Sergeant White from the Lost Property Office was up here looking for you two or three minutes ago, Mr. Richardson. He asked me whether you were the officer in charge of that Chelsea suicide case of Miss Clynes. He'd read about the inquest in the evening paper."

"What did he want to see me for?"

"He'd got something to show you, I think."

"You might get on to him on the 'phone and ask him to come up."

Richardson began to draft the letter which was to be written to John Maze—a letter which was not destined to be sent—when the door opened to admit Sergeant White carrying a bundle of papers in his hand.

"I thought that you might like to have a look at this bundle, Inspector. The taxi-man who found it in his cab last Tuesday night brought it in yesterday, and I happened to see the report of an inquest on a woman of the same name and address that you'll find on these envelopes."

"Did he say who left the letters?"

"He said he thought it must have been his last fare that night, but he couldn't remember what he looked like. He thinks that he set him down somewhere in the Edgware Road."

"H'm! That's not very helpful, is it? Let's have a look at the letters."

The bundle which Sergeant White set down before him was so carelessly tied up that the Lost Property Office had had to put an additional string round it to carry the office label. Richardson untied both strings and examined the addresses on the envelopes. All were addressed to Miss Naomi Clynes, 37A Seymour Street, S.W.3. One of them bore a French stamp. Besides the letters there were quite a number of loose receipted bills.

"You've done very well, Sergeant, in bringing me these. They seem likely to short-circuit my inquiry, but I'll have to take time to go through them. Will you leave them with me until to-morrow?"

"Right oh, but let me have the label and I'll mark the bundle out to you. You see the owner may pop in at any time and ask for the letters."

"I don't think he will, but you shall have the letters back after I have copied the more important of them."

Richardson put aside the draft letters he was writing and proceeded to sort the letters and bills. Most of the receipted bills were those from the milk-shop underneath the flat; there was none from any chemist. For the most part the letters were replies from magazine editors accepting short stories, or enclosing cheques; there was one from Mrs. Crispin, the wife of the Liverpool vicar, and a formal letter from James Milsom's firm, acknowledging the receipt of a manuscript. The letter with the French postage-stamp was postmarked from Paris, and this proved to be of special interest. The letter ran:

> 196 Boulevard des Italiens,
> Paris.
> 14th *May*, 1934.

Typewriting and Shorthand Bureau

"My dear Miss Clynes,

"It was a great pleasure to hear from you again after not having heard from you in years. As you see, I am still in Paris—the only member of our committee that hasn't crossed the water—and as you see, I'm embarked on a school for secretaries, which paid well enough as long as the dollar and the pound were on the gold standard, and there were English-speaking girls in Paris, but is scarcely paying its way now, but I mean to hang on as long as I can.

"I needed cheering, and your letter cheered me, not only because you seem to be knocking the town with your writing, but also because you are thinking of coming over. Of course I will advise you to the best of my ability, as I did in the old, sad days. I am wondering what you have to tell me. As soon as I know the date of your visit I will take a room for you on very easy terms, and we can spend all our spare time together.

"Cordially,

"ANN SIDMORE."

Richardson noted the address in the margin of his report and carried the letter to Morden's room.

"Can I come in, sir?" he asked after knocking at the door. "It won't be necessary now to write to Liverpool for those references. I have just been given this letter to Miss Clynes from Paris."

Morden took and read the letter. "How did you get this?" he asked.

"It was brought with a number of other letters to the L.P.O. by a taxi-driver, and Sergeant White happened to see an account of the inquest in an evening paper. He brought it to me."

"Smart work in the L.P.O. That taxi-driver will have to be seen."

"Yes, sir, I mean to catch him early to-morrow morning before he goes out, and I'll try to get a description of his fare. Then, with your approval, I will get one of the partners in that publishing firm who accepted Miss Clynes' novel to run over to Paris and see the writer of this letter and get from her the letter she had from Miss Clynes. That ought to throw some light on the case."

"Why do you think that he will consent to go?"

"Because he is very much interested in the case, sir, and only yesterday he asked me how he could help me. He is in quite easy circumstances, and he would not think of making any charge."

"The Receiver wouldn't pay it if he did. He must be a rare kind of person."

"He is, sir. Probably you don't remember how he helped us in that murder case in Hampstead"

"Your great case, you mean," laughed Morden.

"All right; you can go ahead provided that he's a discreet person and won't go running off to the Press."

"I can answer for that, sir."

Let me know if you get anything out of the taxi-driver."

"I will, sir."

Richardson went to bed early that evening, for he had to make an early start to catch the taxi-driver before he went out with his cab. He found him at home in Camberwell, just finishing breakfast.

"Are you the taxi-driver who took a bundle of letters to the Yard yesterday? I'm Inspector Richardson."

"Has the gentleman called for the letters?" asked the man, with his mouth full." I could do with a bit of a reward."

"Not yet. What I want is a description of the man."

"A description? I'd give you one if I could, but you know what it is when you're hailed going empty up the street after dark. You don't notice what your fare looks like. He was carrying an untidy-looking parcel in his hand, and he seemed in a hurry."

"What time was it?"

"A few minutes after ten, I believe it was."

"Where was it that he hailed you?"

"It was in the King's Road, not very far from Sloane Square."

"And where did he tell you to drive to?"

"To the corner of Edgware Road and Euston Road—said he'd tap on the window if he wanted me to stop on the way. To tell you the truth, I thought that the gent didn't rightly know where he wanted to go. He was shaky-like."

"Did he tap on the window?"

"No, he didn't. When I pulled up at the kerb where he'd told me to, he was a long time getting out and pulling out his parcel, and then he had to fumble in his pockets for the fare, and he gave me a bob extra and told me to keep it, and off he went with the parcel under his arm. It wasn't until I got to the garage for the night that I found those letters on the floor of the cab. The parcel must have burst open as he was getting it out, and he never noticed it. I've driven some queer parties in me time, but he took the bun. The others had been doing themselves too well—that, one can understand and sympathize with—but this bloke didn't talk like it nor smell of it—he was just what you might call funny, if you know what I mean."

"Which way did he go when you'd set him down?"

"I couldn't tell you that, Inspector. There was a lot of people about, and he just disappeared into the crowd while I was pulling out from the kerb. And now, sir, if you've nothing more to ask me, I ought to start off with me taxi."

Richardson looked at his watch and reflected that it was too early to find any of his seniors at the Yard at that hour: he decided to invade the privacy of James Milsom at his flat in Queen Anne's Gate. He rang the bell: it was answered by the flat-holder himself, attired in a flowered dressing-gown. Before there was time for an apology for calling at such an early hour, Milsom burst out with, "Come right in. You're just in time for a bite of breakfast. Stick your hat on that peg and come right in, or the sausages will get cold." He rang the bell and sent off his man for cutlery and another cup and plate, a second ration of coffee, sausages and bacon. "We don't get a chance every day, Withers, to feed the head sleuth from Scotland Yard. You wouldn't take him for a super-sleuth if you met him in the street, would you, Withers? And yet this man can tell at a glance what you've been doing."

The man looked at Richardson with curiosity, but without emotion. He was familiar with his employer's badinage.

As soon as they were alone Milsom continued, "I've been thinking over this case of yours, Inspector, and I'm convinced that that poor woman was foully murdered."

"You think so, sir?"

"I do, and more than that, I think that you ought to bring in all the possible suspects and put them through it. When you get a really hot case and you start grilling him and he doesn't come clean, you'll have to adopt the old New York Method with a short length of hose-pipe."

"What was that, sir?"

"Oh, it was simple. When the guy stuck out that he didn't do it a sleuth came in at one door with a yard of rubber hose-pipe and went out at the other, but as he passed behind the guy he caught him a welt on the back of the neck—apologizing for the accident, of course—and then, on the way back, he hit him again. After a few times he would come clean."

"Didn't the man complain?"

"Not very often. He knew what was healthy for him, and the hose-pipe left no mark that he could show."

"But in England the police are debarred from asking questions of a man that they are going to charge with a crime..."

"Good Lord! Then how can you expect ever to get home on a case? They've got soft in America now, I'm told. That's why there's so much crime there. They grill their men, of course, but they've gone bald-headed for tiring them out, and for using scientific instruments. In California, I'm told, they use a gadget which they call a 'lie-detector.' They roll up the guy's sleeve and shove his naked arm into a tube of liquid connected with a dial on the wall. When the sleuth who's grilling him asks him a stiff question the blood flies to his head from all parts of the body; the arm gets thinner, and the needle on the dial goes down a few degrees. The super-sleuth's face hardens. 'You're a liar,' he says. 'Look at the needle on that dial,' and the guy shouts, 'Take this damned thing off my arm and I'll say everything you want me to.' That's the modern scientific method of crime detection. I suppose that you've got that gadget at Scotland Yard. Do you think it's better than the hose-pipe?"

"No, Mr. Milsom, we have none of these things except fingerprints, and we're debarred from grilling people, but we manage to get home all right. You see we've got a big machine behind us, and I came here this morning to ask you if you would consent to play the part of a wheel in the big machine."

"Of course I will. What do you want me to do?"

"Well, rather by luck than good management, we have got hold of a letter addressed to Miss Clynes by an American lady living in Paris a week or two ago, apparently in answer to a letter written to her by Miss Clynes. We want to get hold of that letter, and it would be a help to us if you made friends with this Miss or Mrs. Sidmore and got her to tell you all she knows about Miss Clynes. Here is a copy of her letter."

Milsom read the letter with knitted brow. "I see that she talks about the old, sad days. That must mean that she was in Naomi Clynes' confidence. When do you want me to go?"

"As soon as you can, Mr. Milsom."

"I shall have to square things with my chairman to-day, and I can start by the morning boat to-morrow. No, stop! You folks at the Yard always work under a full head of steam. I'll write a note to the old man and fly over from Croydon. You'll leave a copy of this letter with me?"

"I brought it for that purpose, Mr. Milsom."

"Withers," shouted Milsom, "I'm off to Paris in an hour's time. Shove some things into a bag for me while I'm dressing and have a taxi here in twenty minutes. So long, Richardson. Expect me back with the murderer in handcuffs."

Chapter Seven

THE BIG Air-France machine circled over Le Bourget up to time. A taxi carried James Milsom from the airplane office to the Grand Hotel in the Avenue de l'Opéra. Knowing that offices are closed during the sacred two hours devoted to lunch, he booked his room and assuaged his own appetite. At two o'clock he found the office open. Several depressed-looking young women were tapping on typewriters; one of them rose to receive him and conducted him to the principal, Mrs. Sidmore, who occupied an office on the first floor.

"A gentleman to see you, Madame," she said, announcing Milsom, who found himself in the presence of a grey-haired American woman with a very pleasant face.

"I've just come over from London, Madame, on purpose to see you. I belong to a firm of publishers who are bringing out a book of Miss Naomi Clynes. I think she wrote to you about it. My name is James Milsom."

"Is that so? You know Miss Naomi Clynes?"

"I did know her, Madame."

"And I hope you know her still."

"You haven't heard the news then: she's dead."

"You don't say! What did she die of?"

"The doctor who saw her thinks it was suicide, but I believe it was murder."

"Sakes alive! Why should anyone want to murder the poor thing?"

"That's what we have to find out, and that's why I've come to you. You knew her better than anybody else, I believe."

"Well, she worked with our Committee here in Paris all through the Peace Conference, and when the American troops were all demobilized, and the Committee broke up, she stayed with me for quite a time. Say, hadn't you better read her letter to me? I can give you a copy of it if you like."

She went to a nest of drawers against the wall, unlocked one and took out a typed letter. Milsom read it.

37A SEYMOUR STREET,

CHELSEA,

S.W.3.

11th *May*, 1934.

"DEAR MRS. SIDMORE,

"You will be surprised to hear from me after so many years, and I do not now know whether this letter will ever reach you. I am now quite 'on my own,' having at last attained my greatest ambition—to try my luck as a writer. Moreover, I have had an unexpected success in getting my first mystery story accepted by a publisher on very good terms. I ought to be in the seventh heaven, but it is a little marred by a secret anxiety, which may prove to be a mare's nest after all. I need a wise head to consult with, and naturally, remembering how good you were to me in the old days, I turn instinctively to you. When my book is launched I shall feel free to run over and inflict my troubles upon you, if you will let me. I know that one talk with you will show me what my duty is. If you write the word 'come,' will you find me a cheap room not too far from you?

"Yours ever,

"NAOMI CLYNES."

"She had some secret trouble then?" said Milsom.

"In London we all thought that she was the most unlikely person in the world to put an end to her life."

"So she was when she had a worse trouble than this seems to be. You know that she was engaged to be married to an officer who was reported killed in the war. We all admired her for the courage she showed when the news reached her. She just went on with her work, a little more sad, a little more silent than she'd been before, and only once in a moment of confidence did she tell me that life was over for her; that she would have to get over the rest of it the best way she could."

"Look here, Mrs. Sidmore, I want to have a long talk with you about this, and it would take up too much time just at the moment when you are so busy.

Will you come and dine with me at seven or so? I believe they can give one quite a passable meal at the Grand Hotel where I am staying."

"That's just too kind of you. You see I must look after my girls, and we have work on hand that must be finished this evening, but I'll come on to the Grand at seven and I'll take you to a little restaurant where they give you a real cute little dinner. I guess that I can tell you something that will surprise you."

At half-past seven the two sat down to the "cute little dinner" in a restaurant of the second order, where good cooking counted for more than table service. When their orders had been given, Mrs. Sidmore turned to business.

"You know I told you, Mr. Milsom, that Miss Clynes' fiancé was reported killed. Well, as far as Miss Clynes was concerned, he was killed, but two years ago I was taking my vacation at Pourville, near Dieppe, and there in the hotel was a man whose face was strangely familiar to me. He limped just like hundreds of men who were badly wounded in the war. Whenever he passed me in the lounge the impression grew stronger, that he was Lieutenant Bryant—Miss Clynes' fiancé. You see, during the war he was in and out of our office whenever he could get Paris leave from his Colonel, and Miss Clynes had introduced him to us. On the second day I spoke to him in the lounge as he was going through with a Frenchwoman, talking French as fluently as a native. 'You don't remember me, Mr. Bryant?' I said. He stopped short and stared at me. 'I seem to remember your face,' he said; 'where did we meet?' The lady had gone through the swing doors and was waiting for him outside; she was getting impatient and he broke off, saying, 'I'll see you later when I'm alone.' I managed to find out at the desk that he had registered as Wilfred Bryant, and that the lady was his wife.

"Later in the day he came to me alone and sat down beside me. 'I remember you quite well now. You were one of the ladies in that American Society in Paris.' I said, 'Perhaps you remember another lady who was there, Miss Naomi Clynes?' He changed colour and didn't seem to know which way to look."

"What a swine!" broke in Jim Milsom. "I hope you told him so in plain English."

"If I'd said that he'd have taken himself off and I should never have heard his explanation. What I did say was, 'And now I hear you're married, after being reported killed.' 'Yes,' he said; 'I was buried by a high explosive shell, and when they dug me out my death had already been reported. I was taken into a French hospital and the lady you saw this morning nursed me back to life.'

"'And you never thought of poor Naomi who was crying her eyes out? Why didn't you tell her that the death notice was a mistake?' 'I was too much smashed up at the time, and when I got better I thought that a wreck like me had no right to come and claim a girl like Naomi, and I don't know— somehow I let things drift until it was too late to tell her.' 'And so you went off and married someone else?' I said.

"He looked awkward and I thought he was going to leave me, so I added, 'I suppose that the girl had a *dot*.'

"That made him flare up. 'I thought you were going to say that,' he said. 'It's quite true. Her father was a rich war profiteer and she had a *dot*, but I didn't marry her on that account. After all, she saved my life by her devoted nursing.'

"He was very much embarrassed, but I gathered from his manner that it was his wife who had married *him*, not he who married *her*, and if it is any satisfaction to know it, she looked a thoroughly bad-tempered woman who makes his life a hell. To do him justice he had made no secret of his marriage. She goes everywhere with him. He took her over to England and introduced her to his people over there, only— he never announced his marriage to poor Naomi."

"Do you think that she could have run across him in London, and that was what she wanted to consult you about?" asked Milsom.

"That is what I think it was, Mr. Milsom."

"I wonder whether he was over in England at the time when she wrote that letter. There ought to be a way of finding out. Did you ask him where he was living?"

"No, I did not. His treatment of poor Naomi who had believed in him had been so mean that I had lost interest in him. He must have been living in Paris when I met him in Dieppe, because twice during the inside of the week they went off early in their car and didn't get back much before dinner. Now, if you'll let me speak to our waiter we might have a look at the telephone book."

She made a sign to the waiter and asked that the directory be brought to their table. The request caused a stir among the staff, for, as it appeared, the ponderous volume was chained to the desk, and permission to unfasten the chain must be sought from higher authority. But authority seemed to attach some importance to the pleasing of foreign tourists during the financial crisis, and the waiter reappeared from the back regions armed with a skewer with which he prised open one of the links in the brass chain, and bore his prize in triumph to Milsom's table.

Milsom pushed back the table furniture and spread the volume out before him. "Bryant, I think you said the name was? B...B...B... Here we are—'BRYANT, WILFRED, 14 rue Georges V.' Where's that?"

"Why, it's right here in Paris. No. 14 is that big new block of apartments at the corner of the rue Georges Cinq and the Avenue President Wilson. Madame Bryant must be just rolling in money."

"Do you think that I could find out from the concierge where Bryant is to be found?"

"If you think that your French is equal to it. No, I'll tell you what I'll do. I'll go up there tomorrow morning with my business card, and if the concierge tells me that Mr. Bryant is at home, I'll say that I know him and go right up to his *apartement* and ask to see him. I have a good excuse. One of my girls is leaving my school to seek a job as an expert stenographer. I'll ask him to take her name and address and give it to his friends. Then in the course of conversation I can ask him anything you want to know, and we can meet during the luncheon interval. I'll tell you what he says."

"We want to know first whether he was in England during April or May—her letter to you was dated May 11th—and secondly, whether he was in London on the night of Miss Clynes' death on May 15th. Do you think he'd tell you?"

"Not if I asked the questions straight and he had anything to hide, but I shan't do that. I'll round off the corners."

"You're a wonder, Mrs. Sidmore. You ought to have been in the State Department as a trained diplomatist, just as I ought to have been at Scotland Yard as one of their super-sleuths. One of the tragedies of modern life is that all the square holes have round pegs in them. Then it is understood that to-morrow you lunch here as my guest."

"Oh, no; to-morrow it will be my turn to be hostess."

"Unless you accept my invitation right now, Mrs. Sidmore, I warn you that I shall take the morning airplane back to England. Come, be sensible. Promise that you'll meet me here to-morrow at twelve, that you'll lunch here as my guest, and that you will bring with you a note of what you've spent on taxis. You have to make it a business matter."

"Very well—if it will make you happier I will."

Milsom spent his morning in writing out a report for his friend Richardson, reckoning nothing of additions that he would have to make to it before the day was out. At noon he strolled down to the little restaurant and loitered about until he saw the ample form of Mrs. Sidmore bearing down upon him. "Well," he said, when they were seated at their old table, and the waiter had gone to the kitchen with their order, "what luck? You don't look depressed."

"Don't I? Well I ought to. I didn't see Mr. Bryant."

"You mean that he declined to see you?"

"Not at all. I didn't see him because he and his wife are both in London, and they've been there ever since the beginning of April."

"Good Lord!"

"But as I couldn't see *them* I made friends with the concierge who was quite ready to talk. She asked me into her little den and gave me a cup of the muddiest coffee you ever tasted, and I had to drink it too. She wouldn't have done that for you."

"I told you last night that you were a loss to the State Department at Washington. I suppose that you got the lady to talk?"

"I guess I did. When I told her that I had known Mr. Bryant before his marriage, she became interested and asked what he had been like in those days. Then, little by little, it all came out. The poor fish cannot call his soul his own. 'Madame,' she said, 'holds the purse strings, and makes him account for every *sou* he spends out of the small weekly allowance she gives him. The fact is.' she said, 'she is madly jealous of him, and if she sees him speaking to another woman, she makes a scene, and she doesn't care who hears what she says!'"

Milsom began to show the keenest interest. "You saw the wife at Pourville. Can you give me a description of her?"

"She was a thin, wasted creature with hollow cheeks and an ill-tempered-looking expression. She looked sourly at me whenever she passed me in the hotel lounge."

"And they were both in London at the time of the murder," said Milsom thoughtfully.

"I can see what you're thinking, Mr. Milsom. You're thinking that if that woman had ever got to know that her husband had once been engaged to Naomi, she would have sought her out and done something to her..."

"I was. At any rate it seems worth going into."

The waiter came to their table with the dishes they had ordered. When he had retired his clients both remained silent while they ate. The thoughts of both were busy.

"I suppose," said Milsom at last, "that there will be no difficulty in locating this attractive pair when I get back to England."

"It's a small country. The police ought to be able to do it."

"Oh, they can do that all right. The question is how they can bring the crime home to them, or rather to one of them. The fact is I'm not sure yet what evidence they have and how it will fit in with the theory that the murder was done by a woman, but what you've told me may turn out to be of the greatest importance."

Mrs. Sidmore looked at her wrist-watch. "I fear I ought to be going, Mr. Milsom," she said; "I've a lot of work to do this afternoon. Thank you very much for your hospitality. Say, listen! I'll give you one of my business cards with the telephone number on it, and if you want anything done in Paris that I can do, you'll only have to ring me."

They exchanged cards and parted with great goodwill on both sides.

Chapter Eight

A MESSAGE was brought down from the telephone room by one of the operators. "For you, Mr. Richardson." The inspector read the flimsy form.

"FROM Mrs. Corder, 12 King's Road, Chelsea, TO Inspector Richardson, CO.

"A letter from France arrived this morning addressed to Miss Naomi Clynes. What shall I do with it?"

He tossed the slip over to Sergeant Williams who was writing at the opposite side of the table. "Here's a job for you, Williams. Slip along to King's Road and bring the letter back with you. A letter from France addressed to a woman who has been dead for a week may prove to be interesting."

At the moment Richardson was finishing the last page of his report. He attached his signature and carried it in to the Chief Constable.

"This is my report up to last night, Mr. Beckett. There may be something to add to it within the next hour or so."

The Chief Constable took the rather bulky document and adjusted his glasses. "Did you get anything useful out of that taxi-driver?"

"Nothing that I could act upon, sir. He could give me only the vaguest description of the man who left those letters in his cab. The man stopped him at a street corner in Edgware Road and went off on foot. The driver said that he seemed very fussy and nervous."

"Do you think that the fare had found the paper or the letter he wanted while he was in the cab, and had then intentionally left the other papers on the seat, thinking that they would be thrown away."

"No, sir, I don't. I think that, as the driver said, he was shaky and nervous, and he didn't notice that his parcel had burst open and that a number of the letters had fallen out."

"Did you get that friend of yours to go over to Paris?"

"Yes, sir; he went over yesterday morning. I don't suppose that I shall hear anything from him until to-morrow."

"So you've nothing new to report?"

"Yes, sir; I've had a telephone message to say that a letter addressed to the dead woman was left at the milk-shop by the postman this morning and that it had a French postmark. I've sent Sergeant Williams to the shop to get it and bring it back with him."

Beckett shrugged his shoulders. "We don't seem to be getting on very fast, do we?"

"No, sir, but so far we have added to our stock of evidence every day, so I don't despair."

Richardson had scarcely regained his room when Williams returned.

"Well—where's the letter?" asked Richardson.

"I'm sorry, Inspector. I happened to meet Superintendent Oliver in the passage when I had the letter in my hand. He stopped me and asked what it was. I told him that it was a letter you had sent me for-that you wanted it urgently, but he wouldn't listen to me—took it away with him into the registry and said that you should have it all in good time. Of course then I couldn't help myself."

Richardson knew the circumlocution of the registry where every paper and report was dropped into a slow-grinding mill which registered and docketed and minuted papers until hours might elapse before they came into circulation; but, being an intelligent man, he realized that registries are necessary evils if proper records of cases are to be kept.

"Mr. Oliver was perfectly right, Sergeant, and I am perfectly wrong, but if you had brought me the letter I should have broken the rules and stood the racket. Now I shall have the racket without having the letter. However, you must not start following my example or you may find yourself in trouble. The man in charge of a big case has to take the risk of running counter to rules. He must know when to break them, that's all."

As he expected he was soon to find himself engaged in hostilities with the great men who presided over the machine. It was Superintendent Oliver himself who deigned to visit the inspectors' room to read the Riot Act. He had an envelope in his hand.

"I am surprised that you should have instructed Sergeant Williams to bring a letter to you before it had passed through the registry. I thought that an officer of your seniority would have known that all correspondence must pass through the regular channel."

"I'm sorry, Mr. Oliver: the letter was not addressed to the Commissioner. It was brought by hand for me and it should have been brought straight to me."

"Pardon me, Inspector; you seem to have a good deal to learn about the routine of the office. I have been over twenty years here and you have been less than twenty months. The registry is the proper place for docketing all papers that come in."

"You are quite right, Mr. Oliver, but this was a letter which Mr. Morden wants to see, and so do I. It may be a very urgent paper in a murder case-that case of Naomi Clynes. I suggest that you open it here and let me read it. Then, of course, it can go through the registry."

The Superintendent was only partly mollified. "You can follow me to the registry if you like, Mr. Richardson, and read the letter in my presence," he said.

The procession was formed, Richardson bringing up in the rear with a hint of laughter in his eyes. The Superintendent sat down ponderously at his desk, took up a paper-knife and slit the letter open. He called to his second-in-command—an officer of Richardson's own rank. "What is the number of the Clynes' file, Mr. Day?"

"1203 over 77, sir."

Oliver noted the number on the envelope, opened out the letter and inscribed the same number at the top.

"Now you can read it, Mr. Richardson."

At first sight it was a disappointing letter, written by a well-known English newsagent in the rue de Rivoli and dated the previous day.

"DEAR MADAM,

"We have received your esteemed order to which we should have replied earlier had we not taken time to verify the dates of the newspapers in question. We have now traced them and hope to forward them within the next day or two."

"I fail to see that there was any urgency about this letter," observed Oliver.

"No, sir? I am very glad to have it, nevertheless. It is likely to prove an important clue."

As soon as he had left the room Superintendent Oliver delivered judgment. "That young man is getting above himself, Mr. Day. It's what I've always said; a promising detective officer who is promoted out of his turn is a detective officer spoiled."

Unconscious of this criticism Richardson put on his hat and took the Underground to Sloane Square. He found Mrs. Corder in her shop and thanked her for her telephone message.

"That's nothing, sir. I hope that the letter was useful to you."

"It was. I'm expecting a packet of newspapers addressed to Miss Clynes from the same correspondent in Paris. I want you to give me a ring when they come, and I'll run down and take them away."

"Very good, sir. That shall be done."

"Have you had any visitors since I was here?"

"No, sir; none but the Jew gentlemen who came for their weekly meeting upstairs."

"You'll let me know at once if you have any unusual visitors? Good-bye."

When he returned to the Central Office he found a visitor waiting for him: it was his friend Jim Milsom, just back from Paris.

"I've brought something for you, Inspector—something that will make you sit up and take notice. You'll find most of it set out in this report. I sweated blood over it in my hotel bedroom in Paris. I don't say that you'll find every word of it written in parliamentary English. Some of it may be more fitted for the smoking-room in the House of Commons, but you might cast your eye over it. May I smoke?"

"Certainly, Mr. Milsom. No doubt you find that smoking clears the brain."

Richardson began to read the report. It was certainly racy in style, but the matter contained in it was arresting, for it was the first time that an individual had been found who might have had a motive in visiting the murdered woman on the night of her death. At any rate it opened up a new vista of inquiry. This ill-assorted couple, reported now to be in England, would have to be located. It seemed to him to be sufficiently important to justify sending out an All Station message in the Metropolitan area to find out at what hotel they were staying if they were in London.

He arrived at the end at last. Milsom had let his pen run away with him, and the report was inordinately long and diffuse.

"Have you read through that tripe already?" asked its author.

"I have, sir, and I am very much obliged to you for all the trouble you have taken."

"Not at all. I am just as keen as you are to get to the bottom of this business. The first thing you'll do, I guess, is to find these Bryant people and put them through the hoop. You know what I think? While they were here they must have run into that poor lady in the street, or in a bus, or a train. She must have thrown a fit when she saw the ghost of her long-lost one in the grip of an amateur police-woman. There must have been startled explanations and confessions, a mutual exchange of addresses and all that kind of thing and then ..."

"You think it possible that the husband called upon Miss Clynes that night."

Milsom laid an impressive finger on Richardson's arm. "You'll excuse my saying so, but you detectives have no vision, because you read no mystery thrillers as I do. You don't allow for human nature. Here is this wretched henpecked wreck of a man who dare not call his soul his own, and this vixen of a woman mad with jealousy at knowing that Naomi Clynes was his former love. Jealousy like that imparts super-human strength to the feeblest of women—you can see that in some of our publications. Well, they had poor Naomi's address. What does it matter whether both were there or only one—the woman? Remember, she was a Frenchwoman, brought up in the knowledge that if she were tried in her own country the jury would shed tears over her and find her 'not guilty' because what she did was a crime of passion."

"I see that you have quite accepted the theory that this murder was committed by this Frenchwoman, Mrs. Bryant."

"Well, how can you come to any other conclusion? If you count up the suicides in London you'll find that the first idea of lovesick maidens who want to meet their Maker is the gas-oven. The man's is a bullet through the head. Women think that they look better when they're laid out for the undertaker if they've been gassed. All the other forms of death are so messy. Jumping off a bridge is such a cold kind of death, and so ineffective when one can swim. Mrs. Sidmore told me that when she's really roused, this Bryant woman can behave like a fiend; that one night when there was dancing at the Pourville Hotel, and her husband asked another woman to dance with him, she fairly broke loose and created such a scene that the band was sent off to bed by the manager, and the other dancers went off to play bridge in the lounge."

"There can be no harm in my telling you that we have evidence that a man's voice was heard in the room that night."

"Well, then, that woman took her worm of a husband with her to do the fetching and carrying. A fool who allows himself to be henpecked by a jealous wife loses all his will-power and does anything that he's told to do."

"Very well, Mr. Milsom. The first thing we have to do is to find the Bryants and find out from one or the other whether they met Miss Clynes while they've been in London. That shall be done to-night. But before you go I might tell you of one curious thing. One of our witnesses says that she overheard a conversation on Miss Clynes' telephone. She heard her say, 'You wouldn't stop at murder? I was arranging a suicide.'"

"Say that again. 'You wouldn't stop at murder? I was arranging a suicide.' Was that what she said?"

"So the witness says."

To Richardson's astonishment Jim Milsom began to rock in his chair with suppressed merriment. At last he burst into a roar of laughter. When he succeeded in getting his laughter under control he asked, "Are you trying to find out the name of the miscreant at the other end of the line—the man who was putting her up to commit the fatal deed? I can tell you who it was. It was me. We were discussing the plot of her next thriller. Oh, Lord! To think that sleuths were on my track!"

Richardson joined in the laughter and said, "See what a dangerous profession you have taken up, Mr. Milsom. Some day, if your wire is tapped, you may find yourself in one of the cells in Cannon Row.

Now I must leave you and set about finding the Bryants. Good-bye and thank you."

"Stop a minute. When can I come and see you again?

"We shall meet after the adjourned inquest on Wednesday. I hope you will attend it."

"You can count on me for that. Good-bye."

Richardson picked up the report of his mercurial Canadian friend and knocked at Morden's door.

"I'm sorry to interrupt you, sir, but my friend is back from Paris and I think that you ought to read his report before I pass it in to the registry. I haven't had it typed because it has only just been handed to me."

Morden put out a weary hand for the report and glanced at it.

"What an awful hand he writes!" he murmured, but gradually, as he read, Richardson saw him stiffen with interest. "We ought to get hold of these two people before they leave London," he said.

"Yes, sir, I thought that it was a case for an All Station message this evening if you approve."

"Certainly. Draft one, and I'll initial it."

"I've done that, sir, to save time. Here it is."

Morden read:

"To All Stations.

"Inquire confidentially at all hotels whether Wilfred Bryant, formerly a lieutenant in army, aged about forty, and his wife, a Frenchwoman, of about the same age, domiciled in Paris, are staying in the hotel. Important not to alarm them by police inquiry. Arrange confidentially with manager to notify you before they leave."

"Very good," said Morden, initialing it. "What are you going to do if they are found?"

"With your approval, sir, I propose to have an interview with the husband alone."

"Right. Let me know what he says. We have to think about what witnesses are to be called at the adjourned inquest. We must give the coroner a list of them, and Bryant may be an important witness. Who else is there?"

"Besides the medical witnesses there are Mrs. Corder from the milk-shop; Ellen McDougall, the girl clerk to that Jewish committee upstairs; Annie James, the charwoman; Superintendent Willis, about the fingerprint on the typewriter; Sergeant Hammett from B Division and myself. I don't know what you think about calling that member of the Jewish committee, Peter Stammer?"

"The man who went to the office after hours to meet a girl? What can he say?"

"Only that when he was passing Miss Clynes' door he heard a man's voice."

"We had better let the coroner decide that question. You must warn him to attend."

"Very good, sir. I don't suggest calling any of the witnesses from Liverpool."

"No, they can throw no light on the case. But what about your friend, the publisher? Oughtn't he to be called to prove that the woman had every reason for clinging to life? At any rate we'll put him in the coroner's list and let him decide. You have no one else? Very well, then get on with that A.S. message."

Chapter Nine

ON THE following morning Richardson received the promised message from Mrs. Corder. He called Williams, and together they made their way to the milk-shop in King's Road.

"Oh, I'm glad you've come, gentlemen. The parcel that's come for the poor lady is cluttering up the shop, and I thought you'd be glad to take it away with you and examine it at your office. There it is."

She pointed to a very substantial bundle of newspapers tied up with thick string. It was too heavy to carry to the station in Sloane Square, and too big to take into a motor-bus. This was one of those cases in which a detective officer might be excused for incurring the cost of a taxi. They had the urgent duty to examine the bundle before the adjourning inquest. They took a taxi back to the Yard, and Richardson made a note in his diary of his reason for departing from the official rule.

Williams knew not a word of French, but with the aid of a dictionary, Richardson could master the meaning of a paragraph in a French newspaper.

"Now, Williams, you can set yourself to arranging this file of newspapers in order of date. You can do that without knowing any French."

"Yes, I fancy that I'm equal to that much."

He worked assiduously, while his chief was looking through the first newspaper he came upon.

After five minutes' work he spoke. "It's a funny thing, Inspector: all these papers are dated on Christmas Day and the two following days. They are full of very bad illustrations of a railway accident: there are columns and columns about it."

"I remember reading about a bad accident at a place called Lagny somewhere about Christmas last: one train telescoped another in a thick fog, and dozens of passengers were killed. I took particular notice of it because the driver and stoker of the second train were arrested."

"But why should Miss Clynes send for newspaper accounts of the accident nearly four months after it occurred? Was she going to use it for one of her stories?"

"Quite possibly, but I shall know more when I've waded through all this stuff. I remember hearing in Liverpool that her employer's little nephew was killed in that accident, and that his death quite broke up the uncle. Ah! Here's a list of the killed and injured as far as could be ascertained. I wonder whether there were any English names in the list. Hullo! What's this? 'Monsieur Wilfred Bryant and Madame Bryant removed to hospital suffering from shock.' That may be the explanation."

"How?"

"Well, Wilfred Bryant was Miss Clynes' fiancé, and the fact that she sent for these newspapers seems to show that she was aware that her former fiancé, who had been reported killed, was alive. This may have been the first time that she heard that he had married another woman."

With a short break for meals they worked conscientiously at translating the gist of the newspaper reports. Richardson could not help feeling that he was on the eve of a discovery which might prove to be the solution of the mystery. A few replies to the All Station message had already come in. They were negative. When they returned from their hasty meal they found that the telephone operator had piled another sheaf of replies on their table. Richardson ran through them and pushed them over to his colleague. "Nothing so far, but we haven't yet had replies from A and C Divisions where the big hotels are to be found."

He had scarcely spoken when the junior telephone operator entered the room with a message in his hand.

"This may be what you want, Inspector—a message from C Division."

The message ran:

> "Reply to A.S. message of last night. Wilfred Bryant and his wife are staying at Cosmopolis Hotel since April 15th. Manager reports that they have no present intention of leaving."

He threw the message over to Williams. "This is a job that I shall have to tackle alone," he said. "You can make a precis of these newspaper paragraphs from what I dictated to you."

He looked at his watch. Half-past four. It was a good moment for catching hotel guests before they went out for the evening. He set off with one of the French newspapers in his pocket, walked to the desk at the Cosmopolis and asked for Mr. Wilfred Bryant.

"What name shall I give?" asked the clerk.

"Mr. Richardson. He may not know my name, but you might say that I've come with a newspaper." He hoped that the message would be garbled to the extent of crediting him with being connected with the Press.

He was asked to take a seat in the hall while a page carried the message upstairs. The page returned to say that if the gentleman would wait for a few minutes Mr. Bryant would come down. That was one point gained: he would have his interview with Bryant alone.

He waited but a very few minutes. The gate of the lift clashed back and a man of about forty, very thin and frail, emerged from it, leaning on a stick. He looked inquiringly round the hall, and Richardson rose and went towards him.

"Excuse me, but are you Mr. Wilfred Bryant?"

"I am." The man looked hunted and apprehensive.

"Shall we sit down, Mr. Bryant? I'm not going to interview you on behalf of a newspaper. I have brought a French newspaper to show you." He took from his pocket a copy of the *Intransigeant*, and pointed to a marked passage. "I see that you and your wife were in that terrible railway accident in France on Christmas Eve."

"We were, but if you don't mind I'd rather not talk about it. We were lucky to get out of it alive. My wife has never quite recovered from the shock. I don't quite understand why you have brought me this newspaper."

"Only because it had been ordered from Paris within the last week or two by an old friend of yours, Mr. Bryant—Miss Naomi Clynes."

The shot told. The hand which he put out for the newspaper was trembling.

Richardson continued, "You know, of course, that that poor lady is dead?"

He was watching Bryant's face: he saw that this was not news to him. The man bowed his head and did not reply.

"No doubt you saw the mention of her death in the newspapers. May I ask when you last saw her?" Bryant glanced at him apprehensively and quickly averted his eyes. "Perhaps I ought to say that I am particularly interested in her death, Mr. Bryant, and, knowing that you had been engaged to be married to her during the war..."

"How did you know that?"

"I heard it from someone who knew her in Paris."

"You mean Mrs. Sidmore?"

"It may have come from her in the first instance. Well, it is true, which is more than can be said of most of the gossip since the war."

"What else did she say?" asked Bryant.

"She said that you had been very badly wounded in the war and were reported killed; that you had been removed to a French hospital and nursed back to life by your present wife; and...that you married her without informing your former fiancée. That was why I asked you when you last saw Miss Clynes."

"But I don't understand how you come into it. I hope you don't intend to rake up the whole story in a newspaper article."

"Not at all. I'm not a journalist. I am Detective Inspector Richardson from Scotland Yard, and I am anxious to establish all that is known of the cause of her death."

Again it was impossible not to notice the confusion into which this announcement threw the man. He mastered himself, however. "As a matter of fact, the only time I met her was on the day before her death. My wife was with me at the time. I don't think that I should have noticed Miss Clynes if she hadn't stopped in front of me and put out her hand. She said, 'I hope I'm not making a mistake, but are you not Wilfred Bryant?'"

"Did she appear surprised at seeing you?"

"No, not at all. She said that she had seen the correction of my death in the casualty list. Then my wife cut in and asked me who Miss Clynes was. I told her that she was an old friend of long ago. Well, to tell you the truth, my poor wife has been very unbalanced since that accident, and to avoid a scene in the Stores I bowed to Miss Clynes and got my wife away. That was the only time that I saw Naomi, and you can imagine what a shock it was to read about her death two days later in the paper."

"Did she give you her address?"

"Yes, I asked her for it and she gave me her card."

At this juncture the page made his appearance and came towards them.

"Please, sir, Mrs. Bryant rang for me to ask where you were, and I said that you were seeing a gentleman down in the hall, and she said, 'Go down to the hall and tell him that I wish to see him at once, and he can bring the gentleman up with him.'"

Richardson rose. "I'll say good-bye, Mr. Bryant; perhaps you can arrange to see me later in the evening."

"I'd rather you came up, if you don't mind. My wife will never believe that I was seeing a gentleman unless you do."

"Very well, Mr. Bryant, I'll come," said Richardson, who was curious to see this fire-eating lady.

The lift carried them to the first floor where, it appeared, they were occupying a suite of rooms. Bryant dismissed the page on the landing and led the way. The courage appeared to ooze out of his boot heels at every step he took. He opened the door with the hesitation of a keeper who enters the cage of a wounded tiger, and before his wife could utter a syllable he introduced Richardson as the gentleman who had called to see him. The lady seemed to be too much occupied with her grievances to acknowledge Richardson's bow.

"So here you are at last! I've been talking to your mother on the telephone. You told me a barefaced lie when you said that you had been to see her that night—the night after you had met your former lady-love." Richardson became all ears. "Yes," she went on, "I felt it was a lie at the time. I saw that woman give you her card, and you spent the evening with her—your former love. That's where you were that night. Oh, it's no good denying it, and she committed suicide for love of you. It's a pretty story."

"My dear Simone," expostulated Bryant, "this will not interest Mr. Richardson at all."

The lady's voice rose almost to a scream. "It should interest everybody, the way I have been treated."

She was a thin, acid kind of woman with a wide mouth, prominent teeth, and a fire of almost insane jealousy in her black eyes.

Bryant took Richardson by the arm, opened the door and whispered, "I will come down and see you at your office later in the day. I must stay now to pacify her."

Richardson returned to the office in deep thought. Why should Bryant have told his wife a lie about the visit to his mother, unless he had been on a mission that would not bear investigation, and yet, on the other hand, what motive could he have had for ridding himself of a woman who had never injured him. He sat down to write out his report about the newspapers from Paris and his interview with the Bryants. He was still engaged upon this when the messenger announced that a gentleman was in the waiting-room asking to see him.

"Is he a lame man?" he asked.

"Yes, he's a poor-looking fellow, and he limps with a stick."

"I'll go and see him. See that we are not interrupted."

He found Bryant in the waiting-room. He was obviously in a very nervous state. He struggled to his feet. "This is the only time I could slip away, Inspector. As I told you before, that cursed railway accident has entirely ruined my wife's nerves, and her state of mind is making life a hell for both of us. I suppose that you want to know the truth about where I was that evening when I told my wife that I was going down to see my mother?"

"Yes, Mr. Bryant. In view of what happened that evening, I think that an explanation is necessary."

"Well, then, I will tell you the actual truth, and you can draw what conclusion you please. I had written to Miss Clynes asking her to dine with me and talk over old times. I wanted to explain to her why I had never let her know when I came out of hospital. I didn't dare tell my wife—you saw what she was this morning—so I told her that I intended to pass the evening with my mother. The two do not hit it off together, and I knew that she wouldn't offer to come with me."

"How did you send the invitation to Miss Clynes?"

"I wrote a note to her and dropped in into her letter-box at 37A Seymour Street."

"At what time?"

"Just after lunch that day when we met at the Stores."

"Where did you propose to dine?"

"I asked her to meet me at the Globe—a little restaurant in Soho. I dare say you know it."

"And did she come?"

"No. I had invited her at seven o'clock and I reached the Globe ten minutes before the time."

"Did you go in to wait for her? I ask because if you had gone in, one of the waiters would be able to corroborate your story."

"No, I didn't go in. I walked up and down outside, and looked into the window once or twice to see whether she was there, but she never came. At half-past seven I gave her up."

"And you dined there alone?"

"No. I was so sick at heart that I went off and got a snack at Lyons', and stayed there until past ten. I couldn't go back to the hotel before that, as I was supposed to be with my mother."

"Did you go down to Chelsea to ask Miss Clynes why she hadn't come?"

"Certainly not. I should never have dared to call upon her in the evening."

"Are you prepared to make a signed statement of what you have told me? I ask because the coroner may want to call you at the inquest as being one of the last people who saw her before her death."

Bryant gripped the edge of his chair: it was clear that he was frightened.

"Oh, you must not ask me to do that, Inspector. I couldn't make a written statement. I shall keep away from the inquest altogether..."

"You will have to attend the inquest in any case, Mr. Bryant. If there is any doubt about that I shall have to see that you receive a summons from the coroner."

A cunning smile showed in Bryant's face. "I can't attend if I am out of England, can I?"

"Not if you are out of England, but you will not be out of England."

"You can't stop me, Inspector. This is a free country; my home is in France, and if I choose to go home..."

"I shouldn't try it if I were in your place, Mr. Bryant. You may have a most disagreeable surprise if you do. People may say that you were in Miss Clynes' flat that night, and that you were running away from justice..."

"I am quite sure that no police officer has a right to question me as you are doing; still less to threaten me. I've told you that my wife is in a delicate state of nerves—you saw that for yourself—and yet you are trying to force me into some admission that may prove fatal to her reason. I'm sure that that would not be approved of by your superiors."

Richardson felt that this righteous indignation was not ringing true. "I have done no more than warn you, Mr. Bryant, of the consequences of leaving the country when your evidence may be required at an inquest. As far as I know at present you were the last person to see Miss Clynes alive."

"Nonsense; a dozen people must have seen her after I met her in the Army and Navy Stores in the morning. Besides, what sort of a life should I have with my wife if I told the coroner that I had asked Naomi Clynes out to dinner that night? She'd believe anything—yes, anything—and say it, too, in open court before a lot of gaping reporters. I can produce a doctor's certificate that any mental shock might drive my wife out of her mind. Let me get out of the country and have done with it."

"Come, come, Mr. Bryant; pull yourself together. No one here wishes you any harm. I don't pretend to understand *why* you asked Miss Clynes to dine with you that night without the knowledge of your wife, but this I do know—that if you attempt to leave England to escape being asked questions at the inquest, you will be letting yourself in for much more serious trouble than a quarrel with your wife. I must ask you to wait here for a few minutes. I won't keep you long."

To the messenger in the hall Richardson said as he passed, "See that nobody goes in there except a police officer, and if that man attempts to leave the building, shut the door and hold him till I come." He went first to the sergeants' room, where he found Williams. "I want you to leave your present job for a few minutes, Williams. Take your hat and stick; go out by the back door and come in up the steps as if you are a visitor from outside. Get Dukes to show you into the waiting-room and ask you to take a seat. You'll find a gentleman there—it's Bryant. He may take it into his head to bolt before signing his statement. If he does you must say that you are a police officer and hold him."

Williams caught up his hat and stick and went quickly down the corridor. Richardson went to his desk and wrote furiously. In less than ten minutes he had written out the statement which Bryant was to sign.

All was at peace in the waiting-room as he approached it. Williams had pushed back his chair to the wall and was acting the part of the bored visitor to the life: Bryant had slewed his chair round to get a view of the hall through the glass door.

"Mr. Smith will see you now, sir," said Richardson to Williams, who caught up his hat and stick and passed his senior with a wink.

"Now, Mr. Bryant, I'm going to read you the statement which you made to me just now and ask you to sign it. It is quite short. Let me read it to you." He read it. "There is nothing in that that you can object to signing, is there?"

"It's true enough, but I don't want to sign any statement."

"But if you get a summons from the coroner to attend the inquest, you'll have to obey it, and if you refuse to speak when you're called into the witness-box, think of what you will be letting yourself in for. The papers will come out with headlines, 'Scene at inquest. Witness refuses to speak.' You'll be set upon by reporters outside the court to get you to give your reason. They'll dig out your past history; find out about your wife and she'll be dragged into it. Whereas, if you sign this statement, it is quite possible that the coroner will decide not to waste time by calling you. You can, of course, refuse to sign a voluntary statement, for it was voluntary, but I ought to tell you that if you do refuse, you may regret it all your life."

"Very well, then, I'll sign it." He stretched out his hand for the pen, screwed his chair round to face the table and wrote his name in a very shaky handwriting.

"I've one more question to ask you, Mr. Bryant. Do you know the French town of Clermont-Ferrand?"

"I've motored through it several times, but I've never stopped there except to take petrol."

"Have you ever posted a letter to Miss Clynes from there?"

"Never. I never wrote to Miss Clynes until after I met her at the Stores. I didn't know where she was living."

"Thank you. That's all I have to ask. The adjourned inquest is to be held the day after tomorrow at ten o'clock in the coroner's office at High Street, Lambeth. You may receive a summons to attend. Good-bye, Mr. Bryant."

As the man limped out to the top of the granite steps and the door was shut behind him, Richardson went quickly to a window that commanded the street and looked down at the retreating figure. He nodded with satisfaction.

"Is Mr. Morden alone?" he asked the messenger.

"Yes, but I've just taken a stack of papers in to him."

Richardson knocked and heard a weary "Come in" from the other side of the door. Morden's head was half hidden by the stack. "Oh, it's you, Mr. Richardson. Come in. I know that your business can't wait."

"I've seen the Bryants, husband and wife, sir. I've taken a statement from the husband and I want to consult you as to whether he ought not to be subpœnaed at the adjourned inquest as an unwilling witness. Perhaps I'd better tell you what happened when I went to the hotel this morning—the Cosmopolis Hotel." Thereupon he related his interview with the Bryants in detail.

"This statement was made voluntarily, I suppose. Bryant won't go back on it and say that he was forced to make it under threat?"

"No, sir; I don't think so, but I think it right to tell you that the man is not the cripple that he pretends to be. I watched him from the window just now as he was going away. He limped down the steps as if each pace he took was to be his last, but when he reached the pavement and thought that no one was looking at him, he walked away with quite an alert step. He refused at first to sign any statement; told me that he wouldn't go near the inquest even if we served a summons on him; said that he was going to leave London for France and that no one could stop him."

"He mustn't do that."

"So I told him, sir. He pretended that his objection to signing a statement was that he would have a bad time with his wife."

"Let me have a look at the statement. H'm!—unless we have good reason for suspecting him I don't think that the coroner will want to call him on this. What do you think about him?"

"Well, sir, there is an entire absence of motive as far as I can see, but you can't ignore the evidence of that Jew, Stammer, who says that he heard a man's voice in the flat."

"Yes, but there's nothing to prevent the coroner's jury from returning a verdict of wilful murder against some person or persons unknown and leaving us free to go on with our inquiries. We have so little against Bryant that I don't think we need force him to attend the inquest or even to give his name to the coroner as a possible witness."

"Quite so, sir; but his story of how he passed the evening of the murder is rather thin. I admit that if he has spoken the truth in that statement we have no evidence at all. I might mention one very slight incident this afternoon. When he was becoming excited in the waiting-room I tried to calm him by advising him to smoke a cigarette in order to see whether his cigarettes resembled the one I found in Miss Clynes' room, but he took out of his pocket a packet of Gauloises, which, as you know, is nearly the cheapest French cigarette, and he told me that he'd lost his taste for any other kind."

"Well, Mr. Richardson, my feeling is against giving his name to the coroner, but at the same time I don't think we ought to let him leave the country until you have got further in your inquiry. It might, perhaps, be difficult for the port officers to stop him going on board the steamer, but if you let him know that he won't be called as a witness he may elect to stay."

"Very good, sir. I'll ring him up on the telephone and tell him that he won't be called."

Chapter Ten

JIM MILSOM had received a telegram from his uncle, James Hudson, which he dared not disobey. "Meet boat-train at Victoria Thursday. Uncle."

Mr. James Hudson, being a steel magnate from Pittsburgh, accustomed to control large bodies of foreign workmen, was prone to exercise dictatorial powers, but he had a softer side which, if aptly played upon by his nephew, showed him to be in many ways as simple as a child. He had two weaknesses—a horror of being worsted in a deal and a terror of being kidnapped. On this latter subject he was never tired of deploring the administration of the criminal law as it existed in the United States. It was this terror that had driven him to build a large villa in Valescure and to pass an increasing part of the year there. He was a self-made man and he gloried in it. Despite his wealth and the numerous public testimonials to hair lotions he was almost completely bald, and indulgence in the good things of life had imparted to his rather pink and fleshy face the look of a six months' old child—an obstinate child, over-prone to become the bugbear of his nurse.

Jim Milsom, his nephew, knew that the name of Hudson would prevail with the chairman of the board to procure him as much leave of absence as he wanted, and he began at once to make plans. His uncle had always wanted to study English life under a competent guide, and this visit, as his nephew viewed it, was a heaven-sent opportunity.

The train came slowly to rest and Mr. Hudson descended from the Pullman, very broad and rotund, very short in the leg and rolling in the gait. His nephew would have recognized him half a mile away. The cherubic features beamed as he came up.

"What ho, Uncle Jim! Did you have a good crossing?"

"Upon my word, I don't remember. I suppose it was good as I heard no sounds of basins from my neighbours. How are you settling down to work?"

"I love it. The firm is knocking the town. You know, Uncle Jim, I believe I have a nose for crime stories that'll go. I believe that I could write one myself now that I've mastered the rules of the game."

"What are the rules?"

"Well, you start with a crime, a sort of everyday crime that might happen to anybody; then you bring on your super-sleuth. He noses around with micro-scopes and fingerprints and things and spots the man who didn't do it and fixes up an okay case against him. Then you bring in your brilliant amateur, who looks around for the most unlikely guy and fixes on a minister who had nothing whatever to gain from the crime, and wipes the eye of the super-sleuth. You have the trial, a row between the guilty minister and the prison chaplain in the death house, and the execution; only in this country you can't have press-men in the shed when the drop's pulled: it isn't done on this side. I picked a winner the other day—a young woman who'd got the knack; there was a pot of money in her, only they got her."

"They got her? What d'you mean?"

"Murdered her, of course: it was just my luck."

"Did they catch the killer?" asked the uncle in an awed tone.

"Not yet; they've been keeping it until you came."

"What d'you mean?"

"I mean that you're just in time to see how they work on this side from the beginning. To-morrow you and I will go and sit right through an inquest, and I'll introduce you to a friend of mine who is the coming super-sleuth of Scotland Yard. What d'you think of that?"

Mr. Hudson looked impressed. "It's one of the things that I've always wanted to do—see how these Scotland Yard sleuths work. Over in America it's become a scandal. The police are all right, I believe; they catch their man ten times out of a hundred, and then what happens? The lawyers get to work with appeal after appeal until the public has forgotten all about it. Then the judge sends the murderer to the electric chair. Does he go? Nah. The sob-sisters get to work and write letters to the governor of the State and he, poor fish, commutes the sentence to life. Does he die in prison? Nah. His friends smuggle in a machine-gun in a tub of boot polish and he holds up the warder, uses him as a shield, and walks out of the main gate as lively as you please and the whole racket starts again. Why, out of every ten gangsters they catch you'll find that nine of them have escaped from gaol. And now it's not bootlegging, it's kidnapping they've turned to, and if I was over there at any time, they'd have me. Stick me down in some cold underground cellar and feed haricot beans to me till the ransom was paid. There's too much milk of human kindness spilt over criminals in America, and I want to see what they do over here to stop it."

"I'll tell you what, Uncle Jim. I'll have you have a long serious talk with my friend, Inspector Richardson. He'll put you wise about it."

A look of suspicion crossed the baby face as a puff of wind ruffles the surface of a pool. "You've been wasting your time running round with sleuths when you ought to have been at your desk."

"That's where you've slipped up, Uncle Jim. The sleuth came to me to ask me to help him. You see, he found out that we were publishing the poor girl's stuff and that I knew her, and then one thing led to another. When he asked me to run over to Paris for him, what could I do? I had to go."

"Had to go to Paris?" The suspicion had deepened-

"Yes, to trace the poor woman's history. There was no other way. I found an American woman who knew the whole of her story, and that's how I was able to trace the murderer."

"Do you mean that they've caught the guy?"

"They've as good as caught him. They can lay their hands on him whenever they like, but they've got to hold this inquest first. You're just in time to come in for the thrills. We'll have a field-day at that inquest to-morrow morning."

Mr. Hudson purred with satisfaction. "Say, Jim, what shall we do with ourselves to-night? Of course you'll dine with me at my hotel."

"Nothing of the kind. You're not going to any old hotel: you're going to put up with me at my flat. You're going to dine with me at my club, and then we are going to see how London amuses itself."

"No night dives for me at my age, my boy."

"Who's talking about night dives? We are going to a good respectable show. I've taken tickets for this thriller at the Imperial that all the world's going to, 'The Last Reckoning'— you must have read of it in the papers—the play where there's a dinner on the stage in the last act and the murdered corpse is lying in a chest under the table and the murderer cracks jokes about him to amuse the ladies. Then someone kicks against the chest, pulls it out, tips it up, and out rolls the body nicely dressed in a tuxedo. I thought it was the kind of show that would cheer you up, Uncle Jim."

"Certainly, it sounds okay."

*

There was no pressure for seats at the adjourned inquest in the Coroner's Court in Lambeth Road. Besides the witnesses and a sprinkling of Press reporters, there were not more than half a dozen people in the benches reserved for the public, for no rumours had leaked out that sensational evidence was to be given. It was the same jury of nine men and three women. Jim Milsom used the few minutes before the coroner took his seat to explain to his uncle who the various functionaries were.

"You see the tall man over there? That is Sir Gerald Whitcombe, the expert medical witness from the Home Office, who made the post-mortem examination, and the short man he's talking to is Wardell, the police surgeon. That young woman, sitting on the left, is the secretary to the people who have the office just overhead of the flat where the murder was done. I don't know why they've got her here. Most of the others are sleuths from Scotland Yard, but I don't see my particular man—Inspector Richardson. Ah, here he is. Capable-looking guy, isn't he?"

Richardson had been closeted with the coroner in his private room, going over the evidence and deciding which of the available witnesses were to be called. The coroner had decided to cut down the number to the most essential, explaining that, in his view, the jury ought not to be asked to find a verdict against any particular person, but only to establish the actual cause of death. He looked at his watch. "It is time for us to start."

Within a few seconds of Richardson's appearance the coroner entered by the door behind his desk and took his seat. His officer called for silence and the court was opened.

The coroner addressed his jury. "Since we adjourned last week some important new evidence on the death of Naomi Clynes has come to light and will be laid before you this morning. A post-mortem examination has been made by Sir Gerald Whitcombe, the Home Office pathologist, and you will hear some of the results of the police inquiries. Sir Gerald Whitcombe."

Sir Gerald rose and took the oath.

"You received from the police a coffee-cup containing some coffee grounds which was found in the kitchen in the deceased woman's flat. You made an analysis of the coffee grounds. What did you find?"

"I found traces of aconitina—the alkaloid base of the garden plant Monkshood, or Wolfsbane."

"A poisonous drug?"

"Very poisonous owing to the presence of the alkaloid, aconitina."

"Would it be tasteless if taken in coffee?"

"Quite tasteless, until fifteen to twenty minutes after drinking it."

"What is its effect, then?"

"The throat and mouth become parched: there is numbness in the limbs: the power to stand up is lost."

"You made a post-mortem examination of the body of the deceased?"

"I did—in company with Dr. Wardell."

"What did you find?"

"We found traces of aconitina in the stomach."

"Apart from that was the deceased a healthy woman?"

"She was. All her organs were normal, except that they showed traces of the poison."

"What dose would be sufficient to cause death?"

"The dose varies with individuals. Speaking generally, one-tenth of a grain of the pure alkaloid would prove fatal, but there is a case recorded in which one-fiftieth part of a grain nearly proved fatal to an elderly woman."

"Thank you, Sir Gerald."

A juryman put up his hand. "May I ask the doctor a question?" he asked the coroner. He was one of those jurymen to be found at inquests who asks questions in order to be taken as a man of high intelligence.

"What is your question, sir?" asked the coroner, who had had experience of this kind of juryman.

"It's this, Mr. Coroner. If this poison destroys the power of walking, couldn't the deceased woman have put the stuff into her coffee in the kitchen herself, turned on the gas, lain down on the floor, and put her head into the oven? D'you see what I mean, sir?"

"That is scarcely a medical question, but perhaps you'll answer it, Sir Gerald?"

"My answer is that it might have been possible."

The juryman looked to right and left of him, seeking the applause of his colleagues.

"Call Malcolm Richardson," said the coroner.

Richardson stood up and held up the testament while the oath was administered.

"You are a detective inspector in the Metropolitan police?"

"I am."

"You have been in charge of the police inquiries into this case?"

"I have, sir."

"You searched the deceased's room, I think?"

"I did, sir."

"Will you tell the jury what you found?"

"When I searched the room the body had been already removed to the mortuary. I made a careful examination of the floor. Half hidden by the fringe of the carpet I found this cigarette." He held up a gold-tipped cigarette which was handed to the jury for examination. "The tobacco in the cigarette was still fairly moist, and in my opinion it had not long been lying in the place where I found it. On the carpet near the middle of the room and near an armchair I found cigarette-ash which I judged to have been dropped by a smoker sitting in the armchair."

"Couldn't the cigarette and the ash have been dropped by the deceased herself?"

"I judged not, sir. All the people I have questioned who knew her agreed that she never smoked, and there were no cigarettes nor any ash-tray anywhere in the flat."

"What else did you find?"

"Continuing my examination of the floor, I found in the doorway of the kitchen a tack which had been driven in to hold down the cork carpeting. Under this tack I found a minute strand of green wool. I compared this with the jersey dress of the deceased and found that it matched it exactly, and on the back of the jersey I found a little tear which might have been caused by the body having been dragged from the sitting-room into the kitchen. On the kitchen table was the coffee-cup which was produced by the last witness."

"Was there only one coffee-cup in the flat?"

"No, sir, there were two; the other was clean and was lying on a shelf."

"Then the cigarette and the fragment of wool were your only reason for thinking that the deceased had not been alone."

"No, sir; I had other reasons. A portable typewriter was standing on a table, and in the holder was a half-written typed letter addressed to 'All whom it may concern.'" The witness handed the letter to the coroner's officer and the coroner read it to the jury.

"Have you any reason to think that this letter was not written by the deceased?"

"Yes, sir. I have here a specimen of the deceased's typing." The specimen was handed to the coroner. "You will notice, sir, that the specimen is beautifully typed, whereas in the half-finished letter the pressure on the type is very uneven; that some of the characters are blacker than others, and that in two places one letter has been struck over another. I then examined the spacing-bar of the machine and found on it a fingerprint which can be shown to you if you desire it. I took the fingerprints of the deceased. Another witness, the head of the identification office, will testify to the difference between them."

"You mean that the last person who used this machine was not the deceased?"

"Yes, sir. Then I made a search of all the papers in the cupboard and drawers in the flat. They consisted almost exclusively of typed manuscripts; there were no private letters except one from a firm of publishers."

"What do you assume from that?"

"You will have evidence to show that a number of private letters addressed to the deceased were found the same night in the cab of a taxi-driver whose last fare that night had been a man who engaged him a few hundred yards from the deceased's flat. He was carrying a parcel at the time."

"Thank you. Superintendent Willis!" called the coroner.

The head of the identification office took the oath and awaited the coroner's question.

"I understand that the last witness brought you a typewriter bearing a fingerprint on the spacing-bar, and a set of fingerprints which had been taken from the fingers of the deceased woman."

"Yes, sir, I have them here. This is a photograph of the print on the spacing-bar; this contains the ten prints of the deceased's fingers."

"Have you compared them?"

"I have, sir: they are quite distinct. In my opinion the single print is the impression made by a man. I have the typewriter here, sir."

"You might show it to the jury, but I must warn you gentlemen not to touch it, otherwise you may be leaving your own fingerprints on the machine."

Superintendent Willis picked up the machine, took off the cover, and carried it along the line of jurymen who gaped at it much impressed, though all they could see was a splotch of white powder adhering to the spacing-bar.

"John Reeves," called the coroner, and a weather-beaten, broad-shouldered man entered the box.

"You are a taxi-driver?" asked the coroner, when he had taken the oath.

"Yes, sir, I am."

"Do you remember taking a packet of letters addressed to Miss Naomi Clynes to the Lost Property Office at Scotland Yard?"

"That's right, sir."

"Where did you find them?"

"Found them in my cab, sir."

"Were they tied up or loose?"

"They was scattered over the floor of the cab."

"Do you remember picking up your last fare that night? Where was it?"

"A little way down King's Road it was. The gentleman had a parcel in his hand. He told me to drive to the corner of the Edgware and the Euston roads."

"What time was it?"

"About half-past ten."

"Do you mean to say that you didn't get a fare after half-past ten?"

"That's right. I didn't try for one. I knocked off early because I had a cold."

"Do you remember anything particular about your last fare?"

"No, sir. It was dark. He seemed a bit excited and nervous, and when I pulled up at the corner he paid me my fare and went off with his parcel. I found the letters when I got back to the garage and, of course, I took them down to the L.P.O. at the Yard next morning."

None of the jurymen having any questions to ask, the coroner proceeded to address them.

Jim Milsom looked at his uncle and noted with satisfaction that he was absorbed while listening to the evidence of the police witnesses and the taxi-driver who followed them. He breathed heavily when the coroner began to speak.

"That is all the evidence, gentlemen of the jury, that I propose to lay before you. The point you have to consider is whether this woman who, as far as the police inquiries go, had no apparent reason for taking her life, but rather the contrary, did in fact meet her death by her own act, or whether poison was administered to her by another person and she was finally killed by having her head placed in a gas-oven when she was incapable of resisting. If you incline to the view that the death was self-inflicted; that she first drank this potent poison and then put her head into the gas-oven, how are you to account for that letter in the typewriter, typed by an unskilled hand; for that fingerprint on the spacing-bar; for the removal of all her correspondence which was afterwards left in a taxi-cab by a man of whom no good description is available? We have, it is true, no motive suggested for her murder, but neither have we any motive suggested for her suicide. You will not overlook the fact that the murderer, if there was one, took the trouble to remove her correspondence, since that might well prove to be the motive for the murder-- that his object was to remove and destroy some letter which was damaging to him. It is no part of your duty to establish the identity of this man; you may rest assured that the police, whose duty it is, will not neglect it; that their inquiries are being actively pushed every hour, and that in the end the identity will be established. Your duty begins and ends with declaring how this woman died. Gentlemen, consider your verdict."

The twelve heads went together; the jury conferred in whispers; then the foreman intimated that they would like to retire, and the coroner's officer bustled out of the court to show them into their room and lock them in.

Conversation became general. "What do you think of it, Uncle Jim?" asked Milsom.

"It's a good show, I'll admit, but they don't put much zip into it over here. That coroner, for instance, he had the chance of his whole career; he could have drawn tears from that jury, especially from those three women, who'd have burst into tears if he'd given them a little sob-stuff about the poor lonely woman poisoned and gassed just when she had the whole world before her. Those reporter guys would have taken it all down and called it the crime of the century. No, they know nothing about news-values over here. But I must confess that I liked the way that inspector of yours spoke his bit. I'd be pleased to meet him."

The jury were filing back into their seats: the coroner's officer called for silence, and went to summon the coroner, who returned to his desk before they were all seated.

"Gentlemen, are you agreed upon your verdict? How do you find that the deceased, Naomi Clynes, met her death?"

The foreman rose with a slip of paper in his hand. "We find that the deceased met her death at the hands of some person or persons unknown."

The coroner entered the verdict in his notebook and left his desk. The court began to empty itself —the reporters first, hot-foot for the nearest public telephone; then the jury, eager to get home in time for the family dinner, and then the police, returning to their several duties.

Jim Milsom contrived to intercept Richardson in the passage. "Good morning, Inspector. I want to introduce my uncle, Mr.

Hudson, to you. He's very much interested in the way crime is handled here as compared with the methods in America. He has just come over from France." In a lower tone he murmured, "He's a Pittsburgh millionaire."

James Hudson waddled up. "Pleased to meet you, sir," he said, crushing Richardson's fingers. "Say, I'd like to have you dine with us to-night, just we three. Now don't say no, or I'll think that you don't want to get mixed up with us Americans."

Richardson did some rapid thinking. Actually, with the afternoon before him for the inquiries he had to make, he had no valid excuse for declining the invitation, and he was always eager to acquire knowledge of the treatment of crime in other countries.

"I shall be delighted," he said.

"Then where shall it be?" asked Hudson of his nephew. "We must go somewhere quiet."

"Why not my flat? They feed you well there if you give them notice, and my man can wait on us."

"That will be okay," said the Pittsburgh millionaire, beaming on his nephew. "Shall we say eight o'clock, and come dressed as you are."

Chapter Eleven

AFTER A hasty snack of luncheon in the Strand, Richardson set off by motor-bus to Harley Street to have an interview with Bryant's medical man, Dr. Arbuthnot. He counted upon finding him free from patients just after luncheon. He rang the bell and was shown into the patients' waiting-room.

"Will you give Dr. Arbuthnot my card, and tell him that I have not come to consult him medically, but only to ask him for information about one of his cases," he said to the servant, who carried the card away, intending, no doubt, to read the name on his way upstairs with this very unusual message. In a few moments he returned.

"If you'll kindly step this way, sir, Dr. Arbuthnot will join you in a moment."

Richardson was shown into the consulting-room where he was left to himself for a good five minutes. Then a quick step in the hall and a spare, grey-haired man, with consultant written all over him, entered the room.

"Sit down, Inspector," he said. "I hope that you have not come to ask me to violate the rule of professional secrecy."

"No, doctor, I think not, though I believe you will agree that there are circumstances in the work of criminal investigation which would override any professional rule."

"I hope that none of my patients is suspected of a crime?"

"I understand that a retired British officer, named Wilfred Bryant, has been a patient of yours. I need not trouble you with all the details of the case. It is enough to say that a woman has been murdered, and that Bryant has come under some suspicion."

A slight smile flickered about the lips of the doctor—a reminiscent smile. "What do you want to ask me about him?" he said.

"When I had an interview with him two days ago he appeared to be in a very shaky state—very lame and infirm, and very nervous—but when I saw him afterwards in the street he seemed to have got rid of his lameness to a great extent. The question I want to put to you is whether a man in his condition would have the strength to drag the body of a woman from one room into another?"

Dr. Arbuthnot's face had become grave. "Before giving you an answer to that question, I should like to know whether it is intended to call me as a witness in court to give an answer to such a hypothetical question, or do you only want my private opinion, which would have to be given to you in strict confidence?"

"As far as I can say now, you would not be subpoenaed as a witness, doctor. Your opinion would only be treated as a guide to me in a very difficult case."

"Good. Naturally, as a good citizen, I am always ready to help the guardians of law and order. Let me have a look at my case-book to refresh my memory." He took a bound book from the shelf and turned over the pages. "Wilfred Bryant. Here it is." He read for a few moments. "He consulted me as lately as last week. He was then certainly in a highly nervous condition. He said that he had been recently in a railway accident in France, and had not fully recovered from the shock, but from other admissions that he made, I formed the opinion that he had had domestic differences at home, and that these were the real cause of his condition. I might tell you that his wife, a Frenchwoman, is also one of my patients. She, too, was in that railway accident, and is still suffering from some degree of nervous shock. They both told me that the husband had been seriously wounded in the war, and had suffered severely from shell-shock. I doubt whether he has ever entirely recovered from it. I do not mean that he is mentally unstable, but I think him unbalanced to the point of not having a will of his own, and inclined to make the most of his wounds of nearly twenty years ago."

"A man in that condition might malinger to some extent?"

"Certainly. That is one of the symptoms of the hysteria from which he is suffering. If he thought that lameness and infirmity would pay him at the moment, he would exaggerate it, but only subconsciously. He would not realize that he was acting."

"And at other times he might have the normal strength of a man of his build?"

"Well, yes; in moments of cerebral excitement he might show even more physical strength than one would give him credit for, but I should be surprised to hear that he had the courage to commit a murder, and if he did, that he had the tenacity of purpose to drag the body of his victim from one room into another. Seeing what he had done, his only impulse would be to bolt from the scene. But please understand that this is a personal opinion formed rather hastily."

"May I ask your opinion of the wife, doctor?"

"You may. As you know she is a woman from the south of France. Undoubtedly she is suffering from the shock of that accident, but that is not enough to account solely for the relations between the two. Probably you know that she was an heiress and that the only money besides his military pension that the husband has to live upon is her money. Probably she had been jealous and dictatorial for some years before the railway accident. These two people, both suffering from shock, act and react upon one another and this results in very unhappy relations between them."

"I quite understand, doctor, and you may rely upon me not to betray your confidence. I presume that you prescribe for them both."

Dr. Arbuthnot smiled. "I did. I prescribed the one thing that you do not appear to have given him —entire rest and freedom from worry, besides the usual medicine for such cases."

Richardson chuckled at the image of the man for whom perfect rest had been prescribed, as he had seen him last, and rose to take his leave. "I am very much obliged to you, doctor. What you have just told me shall be treated confidentially. Good-bye."

As Richardson was passing through the hall to the inspectors' room, the messenger stopped him. "There's a lady in the waiting-room asking to see you, Inspector. I told Sergeant Williams and he said that he expected you back any minute; so I told her to sit down and wait for you."

"I'll see her in a few moments. Don't let her go away." He hurried on to confer with Williams.

"I'm glad you're back, Inspector. Did the messenger tell you who was waiting for you?"

"He told me that there was a lady. Who is she?"

"She says that she is the mother of Lieutenant Bryant."

"What does she look like?"

"She's a lady all right—an old lady getting on for sixty, I should say."

"All right. You'd better come along with me and we'll see her together."

The visitor rose as they came in. "Are you Inspector Richardson?" she asked.

"Yes, madam, that is my name."

"I believe that you had an interview with my son, Wilfred Bryant, two or three days ago."

"Quite right, madam, I did."

"He says you told him that if he left England something disagreeable would happen to him."

"Not quite that, madam. I told him that he must not leave before the holding of a certain inquest and that if he did he might live to regret it."

"It has upset him very much. As no doubt you saw for yourself, he is in a very nervous state, due partly to his terrible experiences during the war and partly to the feeling that he is under suspicion of having committed a crime. He has told me everything about his relations with that poor woman, Naomi Clynes, and I have come here to-day to assure you that he has no intention of leaving the country."

"I'm very glad to hear it, madam. May I ask when he told you about all this?"

"It was yesterday evening. He made a clean breast of everything. Remember that he is my only son and I know him far better than anyone else could know him. The great mistake he made in his life was to marry that appalling Frenchwoman, but you know quite as well as I do the foolish things that young men did when they were back from the war."

"She nursed him in a French hospital, I believe."

"She did and she has been trading on it with him ever since. Perhaps you do not know how badly equipped the French hospitals were in those days. They had no trained nurses on their staff and had to rely upon volunteers with scarcely any training at all. Many of them volunteered as nurses, not because they had any vocation for nursing, but because they thought the dress becoming. This young woman, my daughter-in-law, was a girl with large expectations. Her father was a prosperous banker and she was his only child. She was spoilt in every direction when her mother died. Every whim was gratified, and when for any reason she was not given her own way, she sulked and made life difficult for everyone she came into contact with. Her temper has grown worse with the years, and now, as a middle-aged woman, she is quite insufferable. I am explaining all this to you in order that you may understand how impossible it was for my son to explain to her why he wished to see Miss Naomi Clynes again. You know, of course, that he was engaged to her during the war."

"Yes, madam, I knew that and I knew also that he did not communicate with Miss Clynes before he married his present wife."

"If you have seen the wife you will understand the reason. She was a very masterful woman, and when my son was discharged from hospital only half cured, she carried him off to her father's chateau where she had him to herself and practically forced him to propose to her."

"Her father's chateau? In what part of France is that?"

"At Issoire in the Central Massif."

"Is her father still alive, do you know?"

"No, he died soon after the war, leaving all his property to her."

"And yet Mr. and Mrs. Bryant live in Paris."

"Not all the year. They spend the spring and the late summer at Issoire."

"But they are not there now."

"No, because after being in that terrible railway accident I wanted my son to consult an English doctor."

"I understand that your daughter-in-law was also much shaken in that accident."

"She said she was, but..."

"You were about to say?"

"Only that I have not noticed much difference in her. Long before the accident I felt sometimes that she was not quite sane."

"On account of her excitability?"

The lady pursed her lips. "If you will treat what I am about to tell you in confidence..."

"Of course, madam; interviews in this building are always treated as confidential."

"Then I will tell you. She took drugs."

"Did your son know that she took them?"

"He could scarcely help knowing. Immediately after the war, when the American soldiers were in Paris, drug-taking became almost a habit. They could be obtained everywhere. I believe that she first contracted the habit when she was nursing at the hospital; that some of the young women asked the doctors to give them drugs and even poison in case the Germans advanced and took them prisoners, and the surgeon was fool enough to give way to them."

This was a new light to Richardson. Probably, he thought, the wife carried drugs about with her. She might even possess aconitina, and her husband might have had access to her medicine cupboard. He saw the pathos of the mother's confidences: in her obvious desire to throw all blame on to her daughter-in-law she was unconsciously injuring her son's case.

"Did you ever meet Miss Clynes?"

"Never."

"Not when she was engaged to your son."

"My son never told me that he was engaged. I knew nothing about Miss Clynes until he confided in me after you had frightened him by your inquiries."

"Did he tell you that he had met Miss Clynes and had written to ask her to dine with him at a restaurant on the evening of her death?"

"He did, but he told me also that she never came."

"There was nothing in my inquiries that need have alarmed him. All I was trying to get from him was an account of his movements that evening."

"Evidently I haven't made myself clear. I have not come here to defend my son against a criminal charge. He needs no defence on that score. My object in coming was simply to explain to you the kind of woman with whom he has to deal. He was not frightened by your questions, but he was frightened at the thought of what he would have to go through from his wife, when she came to know that he wished to meet Miss Clynes again. That is why I have told you so many intimate details about my daughter-in-law."

When she had taken her leave Richardson turned to Williams. "I hope you were taking notes of what she said."

"Yes, Inspector, I had my notebook on my knee, hidden from her by the edge of the table. In ten minutes I shall be able to write out everything she said, but as she's gone she won't be able to sign it."

"No, but I don't know that her signature is wanted. Her evidence has no direct bearing on the case and, after all, it is only hearsay evidence."

"It's a rummy story all the same—doctors in service hospitals ladling out drugs to the nurses on the chance that the Germans might come in."

"It is, but you must remember that at that time people were not so much up in arms against drug-taking as they are now. I know there was a lot of it even among our own troops, let alone the Americans."

While Williams was writing out his notes of the interview, Richardson busied himself over an old copy of the Michelin Guide to France which had been abstracted from the wastepaper basket in the Commissioner's room and had found its way into that of the inspectors.

"Didn't that lady say that the Bryants owned a chateau or something in France? Where was it?"

"I'm not very good at the French pronunciation," replied his subordinate. "As I took the name down it was something like 'he swore.' At any rate that's how I took it down."

"Then you took it down wrong, my friend. In French they never pronounce the aspirate."

"Drop their 'h's' you mean, like they used to do in London before the wireless came in. Then the name must have been ''e swore.' Can you make anything of that?"

Richardson scanned the Michelin map of France with a frown. He had taken Clermont-Ferrand as the centre of his search, and in a few moments his face brightened. "I believe I've got it. Here's a place called Issoire, only thirty-five kilometres from Clermont-Ferrand. You remember that postage-stamp I showed you—the French stamp we found in the jewel-case? That was postmarked Clermont-Ferrand. Williams, I believe that we're getting warm."

Their speculations were cut short. Chief Inspector Farrer, who presided over the leave book, put his head into the room and surveyed its occupants. His body followed his head. "I've caught you at last, young man. This is the fifth time of asking and I'm always told that you're out."

"I've had to be out a good deal lately, Mr. Farrer. I suppose you've come to tell me that you owe me seven days' leave."

"I've come to tell you a good deal more than that. There's no carry over in this department. You can take your leave or leave it, but you can't carry it forward. This is the last time of asking. If you don't want a holiday, say so, and my pen will strike out the seven days you've got a right to."

"I'm in the middle of a big case, Mr. Fairer."

"So is everybody when it comes to the point, but you've got an understudy who can carry on for seven days without bringing down the house about our heads. Come now, will you take your leave or leave it?"

"I'll take it, please, Mr. Fairer."

"Right. When will you go? There's no time to waste."

"I'll take it from to-morrow."

"That's right. Get right away and enjoy yourself."

Richardson looked at his watch. He had but just time to write up his diary and give instructions to Williams before keeping his appointment with his Canadian friend, Jim Milsom.

That dinner at Jim Milsom's flat was destined to be a turning-point in the case, though none of the three diners guessed it. Richardson arrived at the flat at the appointed hour and received a warm welcome. The valet brought in the *apéritifs* without which a French dinner ranks only as a *goûter*. To Richardson's untutored palate the liquid was an outrage, but seeing that a refusal would seem to his hosts a greater outrage still, he gulped it down.

"I haven't been able to keep my uncle off the question of that case of yours for more than five minutes all the afternoon. He won't have it that the murderer was the man we think it was—that man Bryant."

"May I ask why, sir?"

"You may. In the first place there was an entire lack of motive."

"You mean that if Bryant could screw up his courage to kill a woman he would have started by killing his own wife."

The uncle was shaking his head emphatically. "In all the thrillers I've read—and they must run into hundreds—they always start by objecting that there was no motive, and then in chapter thirty-four or thereabouts it is found that the killer had the strongest possible motive for putting arsenic in the coffee. So when I hear you boys say that there was no motive my ears begin to flap. Unless you can establish a motive I, for one, can't believe that Bryant was the killer. If you were to ask the opinion of those who knew him best, I'll bet you one hundred dollars on what they would say. They'd say that he'd have had more motive in killing his wife, leaving him free to marry that murdered woman, than he would have had for killing her."

"Quite true, Mr. Hudson. We, too, always look for a motive. In Bryant's case the motive might have been letters that had passed between them. Bryant is terrified of his wife, who is a very violent-tempered woman, and the murderer, whoever it was, took away with him a mass of correspondence."

"Right! Then if you've got your motive you've got your chain of evidence complete."

"The doubt in my own mind, Mr. Hudson, is whether Bryant would have the nerve to set the stage for a suicide, whether he would not have tried to get away as quickly as he could, leaving everything just as it was, whereas this murderer stopped to write a bogus letter on the typewriter. Besides, Bryant doesn't smoke gold-tipped cigarettes; he's caught the habit of smoking strong Caporal tobacco and can't bear the taste of Turkish or Egyptian or Virginian tobacco. The cigarette we found in the room was a gold-tipped Turkish."

"Well, then, it seems to me that if you turn down this Bryant guy you've nobody left. You're fairly up against it," remarked Jim Milsom.

The conversation was cut short by the valet who came in to announce dinner. It was an excellent meal, such a meal as does not fall to a detective inspector every day of his life, and the wine was as good as the dinner.

"They've been working you hard these days," remarked Hudson. "You look as if you needed a holiday. You're not like this nephew of mine who is holiday-making all the time."

"Avuncular prejudice," said Milsom, with a wink.

"What holidays do they give you, Mr. Richardson?"

"There's a fixed scale, but to tell you the truth I'm in arrears, and I've been warned this afternoon that if I do not take the days I'm entitled to, they will be wiped out, and I shall have to go on to next year's scale."

"Waal, why don't you take them? You look as if you needed them."

"I'm going to: I've got to begin to-morrow morning."

They had reached the stage in the meal when the valet had ceased from troubling.

"If you're going away on leave," said Jim Milsom, "who's going to take charge of this case of yours?"

"My second, Sergeant Williams, will carry on."

"And what will you do with yourself meanwhile?"

"I've been wondering what a trip to France would cost me?"

"It depends on what part of France you go to."

"First I want to go to Lagny, near Paris—the place where that train was wrecked on Christmas Eve. The Bryants were in that train. Second, I'll have to go to Clermont-Ferrand. The dead woman had treasured a French postage-stamp with Clermont-Ferrand on the postmark, and thirdly, I have a kind of presentiment that if I went to France I should solve the whole mystery."

"Suppose that the Bryants were in that accident, what will that prove?" asked Mr. Hudson.

"I ought to have told you that just before her death, Miss Clynes sent to France for a stack of newspapers all describing that railway accident, and I found the Bryants' name among the list of the injured."

The expression on Mr. Hudson's face was the round-eyed astonishment of a child.

"I felt that when she sent for those newspapers," continued Richardson, "it was to find out something she wouldn't like to talk about: otherwise she would have written to her late employer, Mr. Maze of Liverpool, who was also in the accident, and could have told her anything she wanted to know."

"But what I don't see is the connection between that railroad accident at Lagny, and this postage-stamp marked Clermont-Ferrand."

"As Mr. Milsom has already helped us in the case, I think I can go as far as to tell you that I've seen Mr. Bryant's mother, who told me that her daughter-in-law owns a house at a place called Issoire, near Clermont-Ferrand."

"Say, Inspector, why shouldn't we take a hand in helping you to solve this case? I've my automobile in Paris. Why shouldn't we hop over to-morrow by air, have the car meet us at Le Bourget, and take us out to Lagny as a starting point?"

Jim Milsom slapped his leg. "You've hit it, Uncle Jim. Our friend here needs a vacation, and the best vacation you can give him is a round trip in France in an automobile. He can travel as your guest, and what he can't tell you about the difference between the crime problem in England and America wouldn't be worth telling. Besides, I need a little vacation myself."

The enthusiasm in his uncle's baby face was suddenly damped down by this announcement. Mr. Hudson regarded his nephew with cold disapproval. "You need a vacation, do you? Huh! Your life has all been vacation since you were born, but I'll say that you've struck oil in what you've said. If the three of us don't run into something good, well, then, we may as well pull down the shades. What about it?"

Richardson took a deep breath; for the moment he could think of no objection; the oppressive feeling that if he went on leave he would be neglecting his case was lifted: he thanked Mr. Hudson warmly.

"That's settled then. You'll be here by eleven to-morrow, and we'll run down to Croydon together."

They parted cordially, and Richardson went home to pack his simple luggage overnight. He was at the office next morning before ten, and startled Chief Constable Beckett by announcing that his arrears of leave were starting from that morning.

"Who's going to take over that case of yours while you're away?" inquired his superior.

"No one, sir, because I'm going to work on it myself in France."

"The devil you are! I suppose that you've told Mr. Morden."

"Not yet; I'm going to tell him as soon as he comes in."

"Right. It's your funeral."

Morden had not had time to hang up his hat before Richardson was in his room.

"I'm sorry to disturb you, sir, but I've applied for leave from this morning." Morden's face fell. "I shan't be long away, sir, only seven days —and a friend has offered to take me to a number of places in France where inquiries ought to be made."

Morden laughed. "A busman's holiday, eh! Well, I wish you luck, and I wish someone would offer to tool me round

France at his own expense. You'll come back next week with your case solved."

Chapter Twelve

PROBABLY IMPERIAL Airways have never carried so curious a trio as Mr. Hudson, the Pittsburgh millionaire, who was an infant in all matters except his business; his nephew, who was nominally a publisher, and the quiet and earnest detective inspector who was travelling as their guest. It was Mr. Hudson's first journey by air, and he crooned with delight at the sight of the Kentish fields displayed like a chess-board in the sunlight below him; at the country houses nestling in their wooded parks; at the general air of peace and prosperity: and then, as the Blue Channel came into view he descried a toy steamer five thousand feet below him, he turned to Richardson who was sitting beside him and said, "I can't understand how you folks can have any crime to deal with in a country like that."

"England is not all like that, Mr. Hudson. You've seen the quietest part of the country this morning. If you were to go up north..."

"I know it. Little old Pittsburgh over again, without the pep."

"Or the kidnapping and the gaol-breaks," cut in his nephew, from the seat behind them.

His uncle shivered. "Something has got to be done about these kidnapping rackets," he said. "What would you do with them here, Mr. Richardson?"

"We haven't got them yet, Mr. Hudson, but when we do, I fancy that special legislation would be passed in less than a week, as was done in the case of the garrotters fifty years ago, and the criminals would turn to other forms of crime. They don't like being flogged."

"Is that what you'd do with them? Why, in my country all the shrieking sisters would be out if we did that…"

"Yes," interposed the irrepressible Jim Milsom, "and the Governor of the State would get the wind up and give them a respite, and they'd use it to do a bunk. Then they'd look around for a man with a bank-roll—my uncle for instance—and do another kidnapping racket."

Mr. Hudson became immersed in thought as the air-liner crossed the Channel into France and droned over the dreary-looking country near the French coast. He was thinking over the problem of immigration into the United States, and what it meant to the oncoming generation: the flippancies of his nephew passed unheeded.

"It's these foreign dagos that make all the trouble," he said at last. "Why, when they began recruiting for the army in the war, a bunch of men volunteered who couldn't speak a word of English among the lot. Why did they come to America? Why, because their own countries had got too hot to hold them. Among our gangsters you'll find Poles and Italians and Czechs and Russians and Irish, but you can count the born Americans on the fingers of one hand. And now we've let them in we can't get them out. I tell you we've turned God's own country into a cesspool for all the trash in Europe. How would you deal with that problem if you had it, Mr. Richardson?"

"I've never been in America, Mr. Hudson. I shouldn't like to say."

"Yes, but I'm asking you. How would you first set about it if you had the same trouble in your country?"

"In England they don't let the trouble arise, because when an alien commits a crime he is deported to his own country as soon as he has served his sentence. And then justice is swift over here. A criminal is brought before a magistrate within twenty-four hours of his arrest, and if the evidence is incomplete, he is remanded for not longer than eight days: then he is committed for trial and has to appear before the Sessions or the Assizes, which are held within a month, and his case is then finally disposed of, either by sentence or acquittal."

"So he can't hang things up by appealing from court to court as folks do in some of our states?"

"No, Mr. Hudson. He can appeal once to the Court of Criminal Appeal, but that's final, and it takes only two or three days."

Mr. Hudson was plunged in thought. "I can't see," he said at last, "how we could do that in our country. Who would you get to appoint the judges?"

"Couldn't the central government in Washington appoint them as it's done in England?"

Mr. Hudson turned his round eyes upon his companion in frank astonishment. "Shade of George Washington! Why, you'd find yourself up against the cry of 'State Rights,' and at the next election you'd find yourself at the bottom of the count. What would our politicians do if they had no plums to give away to their friends? It wouldn't bear thinking of."

"Well, then, couldn't the prisons be taken over by the Federal Government and all be run under the same rules?—never more than one man in a cell, and regular searching when the men come in from labour, and searching to the skin and cell-searching once a week. You would have no gangsters escaping by shooting their way out if that were properly done."

"'State Rights' again! You would have the Federal Government picking men for wardens who didn't belong to the State at all. No, sir, you'd be striking at the foundations of the American Constitution, and it would go mighty hard with you. You'll have to think up something better than that."

They were nearing Le Bourget. Some of their fellow-passengers were on their feet, putting on their coats and hats, and stowing their passports in a handy pocket. Richardson noticed that most of them were Jews. Jim Milsom touched his arm from the seat behind.

"Do you know any of those guys by sight? They are spending the best part of their ill-spent lives in the air."

"In the air?"

"Yes, and they clear sixteen thousand francs a day by doing it."

"How?"

"Well, it's quite simple. You and I could do the same. The American Treasury is buying gold at thirty-five dollars an ounce, isn't it? Well, you fly over to Paris, go to the Bank of France and buy over the counter as much gold as you think you can carry, fly home with it and sell it to one of the shippers, and there you are! You've cleared sixteen thousand francs on the trip. Next day you repeat the trip. It's far more profitable than publishing thrillers. I could do very well with sixteen thousand francs a day, couldn't you?"

Richardson smiled. "I think that I prefer my own job. But what do these men do in ordinary times?"

"Oh, they scratch up a living as hangers-on at the Stock Exchange—running errands for outside brokers and so on. This is their harvest-time. Look, we're coming down."

It was true. The giant plane was circling over the dreary field at Le Bourget, where they came to rest on the muddy ground. The party let the Jews struggle with the Customs officers before them and take their seats in the crowded omnibus, while they followed to Mr. Hudson's roomy car, which carried them swiftly through the hideous suburb that lay between the air-station and Paris. Mr. Hudson, who liked his creature comforts, directed his chauffeur to drive to the Crillon, the hotel which catered for Americans, and Richardson found himself lapped in a luxury of which he had never dreamed, and at which his simple tastes almost revolted. At dinner that evening he broached the subject of their immediate plans.

"I suppose that we'll start to-morrow for the place of the accident," he began tentatively.

Mr. Hudson looked at him with boiled eyes and continued to munch. With him the dinner-rite was too serious a business to be desecrated by idle talk. "You British detective folks seem always to be in a hurry. You've never had a look round old Paris yet."

"There's no time to lose, Mr. Hudson," said Richardson stoutly. "I feel that every day will cost us a piece of valuable evidence. The railway men who were on the spot at the time of the accident may have been moved away to another part of the line."

"He's quite right, Uncle Jim. We don't want to go chasing witnesses all over Europe. We must back our luck. All the sight-seeing can well be left until we are on our way back."

"Have it your own way, then. I told my man to have the automobile around between nine and ten and he can take us wherever you want to go."

"I see he's a new man, Uncle Jim."

"Yeah; the last man got to sparring with my English butler, Potts, and as one of them had to go I kept Potts because he knows my ways. This man, Adolphe, speaks French and English both."

Richardson had been wondering whether he dared broach the subject of an interpreter. This conversation greatly relieved his mind. "I suppose that you speak French fluently, Mr. Hudson?"

"What's that? I speak French? Not a damn word of the lingo. I thought that you folks at Scotland Yard did your talking in all the languages on earth."

"I wish I did, Mr. Hudson. I can make out the sense of an article in a French newspaper, but that's all: I can't trust myself to speak it."

"Well, Jim here will have to do the talking. He's a Canadian and so, of course, he knows French."

Jim Milsom drew himself up proudly. "Of course I speak French, but the trouble is that my French is the lingo they talked in the time of Louis the Fifteenth, and these people over here don't know their own language. When I talk French to them they just wrinkle their brows and shrug their shoulders. But don't let that worry you. Adolphe's English pronunciation may not quite be described as one of the marvels of the age, but it will do for all we want. I vote that to-morrow morning Mr. Richardson goes down to the car when it comes round and puts Adolphe through his paces. If he gets through with only half marks it will save us having to get an interpreter. What do you say, Inspector?"

"I was thinking of going round to police head-quarters and asking them to lend us one of their men who speaks English, sir."

"One of those guys who wears a brassard on his arm with 'speaks English' embroidered on it? Never on your life! It would fly round that we'd got a Paris Bobby with us and every self-respecting Frenchman would shut up like an oyster."

They parted for the night with their plans settled. They were to motor out to Lagny station, the scene of the accident on Christmas Eve, and question all the railway servants who had been among the eye-witnesses. Jim Milsom was inclined to think that their quest was a waste of time, unless, of course, it should produce some new piece of evidence against the Bryants, but Richardson pointed out that if a police inquiry was to be complete it must cover every possible point.

Richardson was waiting on the steps of the hotel when Mr. Hudson's car drove up next morning. He noticed that the vehicle was spick and span, and that Adolphe wore the detached and self-satisfied look of the chauffeur who takes pride in his car and does not spare the chamois leather. He greeted him in English:

"Your car looks well this morning," he said.

"You think so, sare?" The man's face beamed with pleasure. "I am very glad. She is a fine car." He spoke carefully, but quite intelligibly.

"Where did you learn English? You speak it very well."

"I have been three years in England, sare. I was chauffeur to Mr. Singer. I suppose that I learn English from the other chauffeur. A very nice young feller. 'E give me lessons in the evenings."

"We are going to Lagny this morning. I suppose you know the road?"

"Lagny. Ah, you mean Lagny." He pulled from a little cupboard on the dashboard a plan of Paris and its suburbs and studied it. "Yes, sare; I find my way. Lagny is about twenty kilometres from the Gare de l'Est."

"We shall want you to drive first to Lagny station."

"Very good, sare."

"We have to ask them some questions at the station, and we don't want to take an interpreter with us from Paris. Do you think that you could act as our interpreter?"

"Yes, sare, I think that I could." It was clear from his demeanour that the proposal appealed to him.

"Well, then, the sooner we start the better. I will go in and call Mr. Hudson."

Once clear of the traffic in the Paris streets the big Delage ate up the kilometres and came to a stop outside Lagny station. Jim Milsom led the way into the booking-office as if the place belonged to him and, finding his way on to the platform barred by an official who demanded his ticket, he turned to Richardson and asked him to call Adolphe.

Richardson found the car neatly parked a little beyond the entrance to the station; he beckoned and Adolphe jumped down. To him it was explained that they were held up by a ticket-collector, who would not let them pass to the station-master's office. Adolphe went swiftly to the barrier. They could not understand what he was saying, but the result of his intervention was startling. The Cerberus bared his head, threw open both halves of the door and directed them to the third door to the left. Adolphe had taken liberties with the truth in representing that the foreigners had come from their respective embassies to inquire about the sufferers from the accident and that a complaint of obstruction conveyed to the Minister of Transport in Paris might cost him his job. What Adolphe said in a low voice to the station-master—a stout little pink-faced official—was un-heard by the English-speaking party, but it was assumed to be flattering, if untruthful, since they were invited to sit down. A list of the victims of the accident? Yes, he had a copy of it. He himself had not witnessed the accident, but he had assumed control of the rescue work. Ah, it was terrible! He pulled out a list of many pages from a drawer.

"These gentlemen must understand that this list is not complete because it was impossible to identify some of the bodies."

Adolphe interpreted. "Tell him," said Richardson, "that we are interested in tracing what became of the foreign victims of the accident."

"That should be easy, messieurs. There were but few foreigners on either of the trains." He turned over the pages. "Ah! Here are two—a Monsieur Bryant and his wife—not seriously injured—removed to a clinic in the town."

Jim Milsom became excited. "Ask him whether any of his men saw them after the accident and what clinic they went to."

The station-master flicked over the pages with his thick fingers." Here it is, messieurs! They were seen by the signalman, Jean Herbette, who took them to the only clinic in the town— that of Dr. Jules Colin in the rue de la République. Herbette is no longer on my staff."

Richardson noted down the address of the clinic.

"Tell him," he said to Adolphe, "that those are the people we are interested in."

"Ah!" replied the station-master, "Dr. Colin could tell you more about them than I can. If it had been that other Englishman I could have told you much."

"What other Englishman?"

"The English names are difficult for me to say, but I have the name here." He ran his finger down the column and held up the book.

"Maze," exclaimed Richardson; "ah, yes, he lost his nephew in the accident."

"Quite right, monsieur, and the nephew was buried here. You would like me to tell you all I know about him no doubt, messieurs. He was left lying among the wreckage on the ballast for some time. When he came to himself he got up and spoke to one of my goods' porters, asking him where he could find the children. He said that he had lost his little nephew. I will send for the man if you would like to see him."

"Please do so."

The station-master used his desk telephone. "He will be here in a minute. You shall hear what he has to say from his own lips, and then I will tell you how the body of the nephew was identified." They heard the tread of heavy boots approaching along the platform: knuckles rapped on the door.

"Ah, it is you, Albert," grunted his chief. "These gentlemen have some questions to ask you about that foreigner you found on the line after the accident."

"*Bon, monsieur.*" The speaker was a powerful-looking man in his working-kit. He had the puffy, bloodshot eyes of a hard drinker, but a kindly smile redeemed his face.

"Do you remember the English gentleman, Albert?"

"Yes, I remember him. It was when I was coming down with a lantern. He was staggering about. He asked me where the wounded had been taken to. He spoke French so well that at first I did not take him for a foreigner. I took him back with me to the goods-shed because he said that he wanted to find a boy—his nephew. It was dark in the shed-there was only one lantern—and the wounded were moaning and groaning. I don't know whether he found the boy or not, because I had to get down the line with my lantern, but I did not see him again that night..."

"And that is all you know?"

"Yes, that is all."

"Thank you, Albert."

It was now the station-master's turn. "This Monsieur Maze returned here next day to search for the body of his nephew. He came to this office and I had to go with him, the station being all in confusion, you understand. I had had the bodies of the unidentified children brought into the lamp-room, laid out on planks, and decently covered with sheets borrowed from the clinic and from the families of the staff. I assure you that it was necessary to cover them. They were a more dreadful spectacle than any that I saw in the trenches during the war—indeed, some of the women who were taken into the lamp-room to look for a missing child, shrieked and fainted when they saw it."

"The bodies were mutilated?"

"Mutilated is not the word, messieurs. Some of them were in little fragments. I had got Dr. Maurras to come down to the station to help us fit some of the bodies together—an arm here, a leg there, a head crushed out of all recognition. There had been four identifications when the English gentleman came, but bodies were still being brought in as the workmen were clearing away the wreckage. It was terrible."

"Some of the children were never identified?"

"What will you, messieurs? The fathers and the mothers had perished too. Who was left to identify them? Those that were identified were taken away by the undertaker, but a number remained..."

Richardson had taken out a notebook. "Ask him how many bodies were lying in the lamp-room when the Englishman went into it."

"Thirteen, monsieur—children of all ages up to twelve."

"What did the Englishman do?"

"He made me lift sheet after sheet until I came to the body of a young boy. It was terribly mangled. Then he made me lift other sheets. He stopped long over the twelfth boy and then he asked me to go back to the other. He began to search the bits of clothing that were caked to the body. Suddenly he spoke. 'This is my nephew,' he said. 'I know him by this little scar on his knee which he got by falling out of a tree on to the gravel. I know him too by this undervest which I bought for him in Paris the day before yesterday.' Then he became very sad. 'I must charge myself with his funeral,' he said; 'please give me the address of an undertaker.' The undertaker, Monsieur Rollin, was actually in the station at the moment. I went out and called him to the door, and heard the gentleman give the instructions for a sumptuous funeral in the cemetery. He wrote out on a page torn from his diary the inscription which was to be carved on the stone."

"Was the stone erected?"

"Yes, monsieur, it was. I have seen it myself. You will find it about the middle of the cemetery. The *gardien* will show it to you."

"Did the Englishman come back for the funeral?"

"I have heard that he did, monsieur; not only did he come, but he gave a sum of money to the *gardien* to put flowers about the grave. This, for a little time, the *gardien* did, but I have heard it said that he does so no more, and people who know how much money he received, comment on this unfavourably."

Hudson and Milsom had risen. "Tell the station-master that we're real glad to have seen him," said the former, "and that it has been a shame to take up so much of his time."

The station-master made the usual polite response and bowed them out of his office.

Not a word was said until the party reached the car. There they stopped to consult. As usual Jim Milsom was the first to speak. "Now what about going on to that clinic that the Bryants went to. You took down the address, Inspector."

"If you don't mind, Mr. Milsom, I think that we should visit the cemetery first," said Richardson quietly.

"Good Lord! Have you gone crazy about that little boy?"

"No," laughed Richardson, "but as I'm always telling you it's one of our maxims never to leave any loose ends in a story. Everything must be cleared up as one goes."

"He's quite right, Jim," interposed Hudson.

Get to the bottom of every little thing if you want to be successful; and besides, I'd like to see the grave of that poor little youngster myself."

They entered the car, and as they drove, Milsom asked, "Wasn't Maze the name of Miss Clynes' employer in Liverpool? I thought so."

"Yes, I saw Mr. Maze when I was in Liverpool the other day," said Richardson.

"What gets me," grumbled Hudson, "is that in Europe when a guy has made his pile, and his nephew has got killed in a railroad smash, he should want to have him buried out here in a foreign country instead of taking him home to bury."

"Mr. Maze didn't strike me as a man of sentiment," explained Richardson. "As a lawyer he may have thought that one country it as good as another for getting buried in."

"Did he tell you about having lost his nephew?"

"I heard from other people in Liverpool that he was frightfully upset so I didn't refer to it."

The cemetery at Lagny lay on rising ground a quarter of a mile outside the town. It was the local luncheon hour, and they found the guardian less communicative than he might have been at another hour of the day. But Adolphe would stand no nonsense. For foreigners of this distinction, backed by their embassies, all restrictions must give way. Rather sulkily the man unlocked the gate, pointed to a tall limestone cross and left the visitors to find their own way to it.

The cross was well cut; a few withered flowers stood in a pot on the grave—a point that was not unnoticed by Adolphe. The others were bending over the inscription which Richardson was copying into his notebook. It was in English.

SACRED TO THE MEMORY OF

GODFREY MAZE

WHO WAS KILLED IN A RAILWAY

ACCIDENT AT LAGNY ON 24TH

DECEMBER, 1933

Aged 9 years

The *gardien* emerged from his lodge, wiping his mouth. Adolphe stopped to engage him in conversation, while his party went on to the car. They observed that the man was spreading his palms out in the gesture of self-justification. Adolphe came from the gate at a run.

"What was it, Adolphe?" asked his master.

"Excuse me, sir. I was asking the man what he meant by neglecting that grave when he had been paid for looking after it. I ventured to tell him that he would hear more of it."

Chapter Thirteen

THE CLINIC in the rue de la République was kept by the most eccentric-looking doctor that any of them had seen. They were shown into the *parlour*; the door flew open and a bearded figure burst in and stopped short. They rose politely. He looked for all the world like an anthropoid ape, badly in need of washing and grooming. His face was hirsute; his clothing—riding-breeches, gaiters and all—was fit only to be thrown into the municipal destructor. His little eyes were bright and full of intelligence.

"Well, gentlemen; your business, if you please? I, myself, am a very busy man."

"Tell him," said Milsom, addressing Adolphe, "that we have come to inquire about two English people who were injured in the railway accident on Christmas Eve."

Adolphe put the question in French.

"Ah! Then these gentlemen speak no French? They are English?—Countrymen of Monsieur Bryant. Doubtless they are come to tell me that he has done it at last."

"Done what?" asked Milsom, when the reply was translated.

"*Eh, bien!* Swallowed the dose that he had always carried in his pocket—the cyanide of potassium. No? Then what poison did he use? It interests me to know."

"Tell him," said Milsom impatiently, "that we saw him alive and well in London last week."

"Then why have these gentlemen come—to hear my impressions of Monsieur Bryant and his wife? Good! I will tell them. They were quite uninjured by the accident, but they had been badly shaken. The lady in particular was a difficult case. She complained of everything—the nurses, the food, her mattress—everything. If she suffered from anything it was hypochondriasis and ill-temper. We were glad to be rid of her. As for the poor husband, I pitied him. When the nurse found that little bottle of cyanide in his pocket, I pitied him the more. I thought at first that he was the victim of stupefying drugs, but it was not that. He told me that he carried the cyanide with him for months as a method of escape from his wife, but he had always lacked the courage to use it—even the courage to put his head into a gas-oven. I told him that death was but a little thing—that people met death face to face every day, and that the world was not one sou the worse when they left it. He said that he had faced death in the trenches when he was younger, and that now when he wished for it, he did not dare to die. I told him that he was wise; that one never knew what was waiting for one round the corner—good fortune, perhaps. He sighed and said that if anything would be waiting round the corner for him, it would be his wife."

The doctor flashed upon them what was intended to be a smile, it was an exhibit of ragged yellow teeth. "Ah, messieurs, what will you, he was a neurotic; a victim of shell-shock nearly twenty years ago; there are many like him."

"Ask him what became of them."

"Oh, I bundled them both out of the clinic on the third day. Their beds were wanted for more serious cases than theirs. You tell me that they went to England? That surprises me when I remember that the wife was a Frenchwoman; and he told me that it was she who possessed the fortune. Now, messieurs, if you have no other questions to put to me, I will ask you to set me free: my patients are waiting for me."

They thanked the doctor and were glad to escape from his overpowering presence.

In the car, on their way to lunch, Milsom remarked, "I should like to have had that guy taken to a Turkish bath, had him shaved and his hair cut, burnt his clothes and sent him out as a civilized man."

"Huh!" growled his uncle, "and he'd have lost all his practice; his appearance is half his stock-in-trade."

Lagny is not a town that lends itself to gastronomy. The Moulin Bleu in the Allée Antoinette was Adolphe's choice. They ate their lunch on the verandah which commanded a good view.

The food was excellent. Between the courses Jim Milsom felt free to express his views.

"Well, we haven't wasted our time here, have we? Now that we know from that chimpanzee doctor the kind of guy this Bryant is, we can go straight ahead. Carried poison about with him in his pocket; talked about sticking his head in a gas-oven. Why, there you are."

"And the motive?" asked Richardson, with a twinkle.

"Oh, we know about the motive. She had been his fiancée; he went to her flat to get her to run away with him; she turned him down and then, of course, for a man in that state of nerves it was only a step to the poison and the gas-oven. He was afraid of them for himself, but they were all right for other people. What do you think, Uncle Jim?"

Mr. Hudson was never profuse, either in brain-work or words, when he was eating. He waved a fat hand towards his nephew and took another mouthful.

"My uncle won't commit himself, Inspector, but you see what I mean?"

"I do, Mr. Milsom."

"But I see you're not convinced."

"I should like to get a little further into the case before forming an opinion. I remember what his mother told me—that it was his wife who took drugs and carried poison about with her, but he seems to have told the doctor that the habit was his; perhaps the mother was trying to shield him."

"Well, now that we are full-fed, we won't waste our time in this hole. What about pushing off to Clermont-Ferrand?"

"Pardon me, I should like to make a few more inquiries this afternoon."

"What! You don't want to see that chimpanzee again?"

"No, I want to see one or two of those railway-men, I want to find out from them where Mr. Maze slept on the night of the accident, and then go on to Clermont-Ferrand."

Mr. Hudson woke to activity. "Say, if you're not going straight back to Paris I'll have to get back this afternoon and cash a traveller's cheque at the American Express Company. I'll take the car and be back before five."

"Then you'll need Adolphe to drive you. What will Mr. Richardson do without an interpreter?" asked Milsom. "I'll tell you what, Uncle Jim. I'll drive you."

His uncle shuddered. "I'm getting an old man, Jim. My nerves are not what they were. With you at the wheel..."

"That was before I became a publisher. I don't drive like that now. Why, the other day a truck-driver in England who'd been hooting to pass me, asked me what firm of undertakers employed me. No, I'll run you up to Paris and keep you looking at your watch all the way."

So it was arranged. Richardson and Adolphe watched uncle and nephew start, and then they walked down to the station for a second interview with the station-master, who received them with the same deference as in the morning. Richardson took the seat that was offered him and opened his business.

"We have seen the grave of Mr. Maze's little boy, monsieur, but there is one question that we forgot to ask you. Where did Mr. Maze pass the night after the accident?"

"I cannot answer that question, monsieur, but I can tell you one thing that may be useful to you. Most of the passengers who were not too badly injured engaged cars from the garage nearly opposite the station. The garagist may be able to tell you where the Englishman went."

Richardson rose. "Thank you, monsieur. It is, after all, a very small point, but I should like to clear it up. The garage is opposite the station?"

"Yes, monsieur; not exactly opposite, but a hundred yards distant in the direction of the town. Milleaud is the name."

"Now we'll go to that garage, Adolphe, and you will ask the garagist where he was ordered to drive Mr. Maze, if it was Mr. Maze."

"I understand, monsieur. First I must get a description of the gentleman in order to be sure that it was the same man, and then I must ask where he went."

Milleaud, the garagist, was in his little cubby-hole of an office, casting up his accounts. Richardson loitered outside to give his interpreter a free hand. Adolphe explained his business, saying that some highly-placed English had come out from London to trace an Englishman who had been in the accident on Christmas Eve; that the station-master had told them that he might have come to the garage shortly after the accident to engage a car.

"My cars were all engaged that night, driving the injured to one place or another," explained Milleaud. "Each paid for his car at the time. It is difficult to remember any one in particular."

"But this was a foreigner—an Englishman."

Milleaud lifted his shoulders. "All my clients that evening spoke French. Stop! There was one who spoke with some accent—English it might have been. He was the last to come here that night."

"Can you describe him?"

Milleaud searched his memory. "He was a big man—I remember that—and getting on in years, I should say. The hair that showed under his hat looked grey in the lamplight. That is all I can remember about him. He was so persistent about having a car to drive him that in the end I gave way, and drove him myself."

"Where did you drive him to?"

"To Nogent-sur-Marne. You see, the clinic here was full. He asked me what was the nearest town which had a clinic, and of course I said Nogent. He asked me whether the doctor-in-charge of it was a good man, and I told him quite truly that Dr. Guillaume had a reputation extending far beyond Nogent. I ran out the car, and he picked up the little boy and lifted him in..."

"What little boy? I thought that he came to you alone."

"Didn't I tell you that he had a little boy with him? He had carried him over from the station in his arms. Little, did I say? He was not so very little—a boy of eight or nine, I should think. His head was bandaged and was lying on the gentleman's shoulder. I got out of the car and held the boy while he got in. Then I lifted the boy into his arms on the back seat, and we drove off. When we reached the clinic at Nogent we were told that other wounded had arrived—that there was only one vacant bed, so the boy was taken in and the gentleman got me to drive him to the Hotel de France for the night. I left him there."

"Excuse me for a moment," said Adolphe. "I have a friend who speaks no French waiting outside. I should like to tell him what you say." To Richardson, who was waiting outside the little office, he repeated the conversation.

"He said that the man had a wounded boy with him? Then it cannot have been Mr. Maze."

"Yet the description he gave of him—a tall Englishman of middle age who spoke French fluently—seemed to fit Mr. Maze." Adolphe turned to the garage proprietor who had joined them. "You say that that gentleman spoke with an English accent?"

"It seemed to me that the accent was English, monsieur."

"Ask him how far it is to Nogent."

"I can tell you that, sir. It is eighteen kilometres."

Richardson consulted his watch. "Then we've time to go there before the others get back. Ask him what he would charge for driving us out, there and back?"

The garagist had met his match in the art of bargaining. Adolphe beat him down to a franc and a half a kilometre for the double journey, and hinted at a liberal *pourboire*.

Richardson made a mental survey of his private resources and decided that it was worth while. "Very well, Adolphe. Tell him to get out the car and we'll start straight away."

It was a fairly open road to Nogent-sur-Marne, and the car covered the distance in twenty minutes. They drove straight to the nursing-home: the two passengers went in, leaving the car to wait outside. They were received by the matron. Adolphe explained that they had come to inquire about a little English boy who had been injured in the railway accident at Lagny.

"Ah, yes, messieurs, I remember him well."

"Is he still here?"

"No, messieurs; his father called for him the next afternoon and took him away in a car."

"But was he well enough to travel?"

"Dr. Guillaume seemed to think it unwise, but what will you? We have no power to detain our patients except, perhaps, in very grave cases."

"May we have a word with Dr. Guillaume?"

"Certainly, messieurs. I will call him."

In less than two minutes the door opened to admit a young-looking doctor with a gravity beyond his years.

"You have called about that little English boy who was injured in the Lagny accident, yes?"

"Yes, monsieur," answered Adolphe.

"Well, his father took him away the next day, against my advice."

"Was he too ill to travel?"

"Physically, he was not too ill to travel a moderate distance, but he was suffering from shock, and he seemed to have lost all memory of what had happened up to the time of the accident.

One of our nurses speaks English and that is what she reported to me. I should be interested to hear how he is now. The impression I formed was that he would never recover his memory. I told the father this when he insisted on taking him away."

"Were the head injuries serious?"

Dr. Guillaume pursed his lips. "I cannot say that. He had received a blow—that was evident from the bruise—but there was no question of a serious concussion of the brain. He was, as I told his father, fit to travel a moderate distance without ill effects."

"Did the father say where he was taking him?"

"No, he was curiously reticent when I asked him. He replied evasively that it would be less than fifty kilometres. May I ask whether this gentleman is a relative of Monsieur Godfrey."

"Monsieur Godfrey!" said Adolphe. "Did he give his name as Godfrey?"

"Yes."

Adolphe turned to Richardson. "This cannot be the gentleman you are inquiring about. This one gave his name as Godfrey, not Maze."

Richardson held up his hand to check him. "The doctor asks whether I am a relative of Mr. Godfrey. Tell him that I am not, but that I am acquainted with him; that I have come to France to find him if I can."

Adolphe translated the reply. The doctor seemed surprised. "I knew that Monsieur Godfrey had been severely shaken by the accident. He told me that he had lost consciousness for some moments, but we had no vacant bed here to offer him and he went to the hotel for the night. When he called to take his son away he was perfectly normal."

"Did he take him away in a car?"

"So they told me. I did not see it myself; they may be able to tell you something at the Hotel de France."

To the Hôtel de France they went. The woman at the desk had a vivid recollection of the accident, but only a hazy one about visitors to the hotel so many months before. "An English gentleman, you say?" She shook her head. "We have had no English visitors for months past. It is on account of the rate of exchange, they say."

"This Englishman spoke fluent French; he may have registered in the name of 'Godfrey.'"

"That will mean perhaps two hours of searching in the books."

"But I will relieve madame of the searching," said Adolphe gallantly. "I could do it here under your own eyes if you would give me the book for last Christmas."

The lady produced the book from a shelf behind her; Adolphe and Richardson pored over it. "Here it is!" cried Richardson. "John Godfrey. Room 37."

Adolphe announced their discovery to the lady at the desk. "Would it be possible, madame, to ascertain how the gentleman left the hotel—whether by train or by car?"

The lady threw out her hands in dismay. "Ascertain how a client of four months ago left the hotel? Impossible, messieurs!"

Richardson had noticed a bright-eyed boy in uniform, listening to the conversation with intense interest. He looked as if he was bursting to join in. He touched Adolphe on the arm. "I believe that boy could tell us something. Let us get him away from the desk."

Adolphe thanked the woman profusely and led the way towards the door. The chasseur scurried past him to open it and followed the two men out to the doorstep. Adolphe began to question him.

"I can see that you remember all about that railway accident at Lagny, my boy. Perhaps you remember that Englishman we were talking about."

"I do, monsieur. I carried his bag up to his room. The next morning when I brought him his breakfast he asked me about the train to Lagny. I told him. You see, I know them all by heart. He went off to the station after breakfast, and when he came back at four o'clock to pay his bill and get his valise, he was in one of Monsieur Braudon's cars from the garage near the station. One of the garage hands whom I know well—Jean Ravel—was driving."

"Is he still at the garage?"

"Yes, monsieur; he'll be able to tell you where he went that afternoon."

Richardson further depleted his dwindling funds by slipping a five-franc piece into the boy's palm, the guerdon of an excellent memory. They jumped into their car and drove down to the garage. Fortunately Jean Ravel was busy oiling a customer's car. He remembered the incident perfectly.

"The gentleman picked up his valise, paid his bill and told me to drive to Dr. Guillaume's clinic. There he kept me waiting for perhaps a quarter of an hour. Then one of the nurses helped him to carry out a boy with a bandaged head, and the gentleman ordered me to drive to Orleans. When we neared the town he told me to stop at a chemist's to ask the address of a clinic. I drove him to that clinic. It was in the rue des Orfévres. There he paid me off and I left him."

Richardson had been making rapid notes. He looked at his watch and saw that it was half-past four. "We must get back," he said.

They were deposited at the Moulin Bleu where Adolphe insisted upon offering his companion an *apèritif*. They were half through it when Adolphe cocked his ear. He knew the purr of his car as a mother knows the whimper of her infant. "Hark! They have returned," he said, swallowing the remainder of his *apèritif* at a gulp.

Both uncle and nephew seemed to be pleased with the world. The uncle had cashed his cheque and seemed ready for the conquest of France, but less ready perhaps to admit that his nephew was the most prudent driver of his experience. There was a friendly exchange of badinage between them on this point.

"Now," said Mr. Hudson, "when we've had a drink we'll be ready to start for any place, Inspector."

"We must go to Orleans, if you don't mind, Mr. Hudson."

"To Orleans? What's the great idea?"

"Well, sir, since you've been away we have been over to Nogent-sur-Marne and I think that we've made a discovery."

Chapter Fourteen

MR. HUDSON's beverage was tea; Richardson pointed mutely to his unemptied glass; Jim Milsom ordered something more potent and exhilarating. "Now, Inspector, let us hear all about your discovery," he said, when the waiter had left them to themselves.

"Well, sir, we found that an Englishman, whose description tallied closely with that of John Maze, ordered a car from the garage near the station on the night of the accident and drove to Nogent-sur-Marne with a small boy who appeared to have been in the accident because his head was bandaged. He took this boy to the clinic at Nogent and told the people there that he was his son, but the strangest part of the story is that he gave his name on this occasion as John Godfrey."

"It must have been another Englishman," said Hudson.

"I think not, sir. The station-master was positive that there were only two Englishmen on that train, John Maze and Wilfred Bryant."

"Perhaps he got a blow on the head, too, and didn't know what he was saying. There have been cases in America of men forgetting their own names."

"I thought of that, Mr. Hudson, but the doctor described him as being perfectly normal, and when the man identified that body and gave instructions to the undertaker he called himself Maze."

"Say, he may have been travelling with two boys when he left Paris."

"He said nothing to the station-master about there being two."

"No, that's so. Waal, so you followed him out to Nogent."

"How did you go?" asked Milsom.

"We hired a car, sir, and kept it until we had finished our inquiry."

"You'll be able to recover the money from Scotland Yard when you get home?"

Richardson looked embarrassed. "I'm afraid not, sir, but that's of no consequence."

"No such thing, Inspector. This is our show, and we won't have you putting your hand in your pocket till it's over. Tell Adolphe what you spent and he'll refund it out of his expense account."

"Thank you very much, sir; it's very kind of you."

"What I'm dying to know," said Milsom, "is what they told you at that clinic in Nogent."

"It wasn't only at the clinic that I got information. I got it from the hotel and a garage in the town. The man who called himself Godfrey returned to the clinic next morning with a car and told the doctor that he proposed to take the boy away. The doctor objected that it might be dangerous to the child's health, but as the boy was conscious, he could not, of course, detain him. The boy had, it seems, entirely lost his memory, and the doctor seemed to think it doubtful whether he would ever recover it. At the hotel I learned that he took the child to Orleans."

"How far is Orleans?"

"About one hundred kilometres, sir. We ought to be able to do it comfortably in an hour and a half."

"Have you the address of the clinic there?"

"Yes, sir; it is in the rue des Orfévres. I have seen the man who drove them to Orleans. Mr. Godfrey, as he called himself, carried the boy into the clinic and paid off the car."

"Certainly it's funny. This man identifies and buries his nephew here, and then motors off with another boy supposed to be his son, and under another name. Had he two boys with him—a son and a nephew—and was he trying to foist the nephew in the place of his son who was killed?"

"No, sir, Mr. Maze is a bachelor and has no son."

"I'll tell you what, Uncle Jim; the inspector has ferreted out material for a top-hole thriller."

"The first thing we've got to clear up is this," said Richardson. "Is the man we are following Mr. Maze, or another Englishman altogether? Are there two men or one? And if only one, why so many clinics?"

"Yes, you've struck the weak point in the thriller," said Milsom. "If the guy was out to cover up his tracks one could understand him changing his name, but why so many clinics?"

"Well, we won't solve the puzzle by sitting here talking," declared Hudson, signalling to the waiter.

"We'd best be getting along."

They found Adolphe immersed in his *Michelin* Guide. "You know the way to Orleans?" asked his employer.

"Yes, sir."

"Step on the gas then, Adolphe, and let us get on with it."

Adolphe "stepped on the gas," and the car went like the wind. Mr. Hudson belonged to the class of motor-owners who have a childlike confidence in the skill of any driver who wears a uniform, but a pathetic mistrust of every driver in mufti, drive he never so carefully.

They found themselves at Orleans before six, and were driven straight to the clinic.

"We can't invade this clinic in body," said Milsom; "we'd scare the little sisters out of their wits. What about Mr. Richardson, with Adolphe to interpret for him, breaking the ground first, while we stop in the car?"

"Okay, but push on with it."

"Right, Uncle; in thrillers like this is there mustn't be a hitch for a moment in unrolling the evidence."

Richardson rang the bell, and Adolphe asked the sister in uniform who opened the door whether they could see the doctor.

"On the subject of...?"

"On the subject of a young English boy who was admitted as a patient immediately after the railway accident at Lagny."

The sister's face broke into a smile. "I remember that little boy well," she said, and tripped down the passage.

A moment later the doctor made his appearance and to Richardson's relief addressed them in excellent English.

"You are asking about an English boy who was here four or five months ago? Godfrey was his name."

"Yes," said Richardson. "My friends and I are anxious to know what became of him."

"Ah! And I, too, would like to know. We became much attached to that boy; he was a dear little fellow."

"Was he seriously injured?"

"I cannot say that. He had received a blow on the head which left a big bruise, and he was suffering from shock, but his physical condition was unaffected by it. He slept and ate well; he could laugh and joke with me and with the sisters, but he had lost his memory. He did not even appear to know his own father, and he had no recollection of the accident or of anything that preceded it. During the war this was not uncommon among men suffering from shell-shock."

"Did they recover their memory?" asked Richardson.

"In most cases, yes, but not in all, and that is why I am sorry that I could not follow up this particular case. The boy was so lively and intelligent, so quick in noticing things, that I should have expected that he would entirely recover. But..."

"Did his father take him away?"

"He did, and after only six days in the clinic. It should have been longer."

"Where did they go?"

The doctor spread his two hands out from the elbow. "The father did not say where he was taking him. He was curiously reticent about his destination. He called for the boy in a car, and I presumed that he was taking him back to England."

"He has never written to you since?"

"No. Of course, as he had paid the account, he was not constrained to write, though most people do send a line of gratitude, particularly the English."

"Thank you very much, doctor," said Richardson, rising. "I ought to explain why I have troubled you. It is because my friends who are waiting below knew that the boy had been here, and thought that you might be able to give them his present address."

"I wish I knew it," replied the doctor, shaking hands. "If you hear where he is, you will give much pleasure to our nurses if you will write to me."

"One more question, doctor. Did the father stay here?"

"No, he stayed at the Hôtel Métropole."

Richardson returned to the car and reported his conversation.

"Okay," said Mr. Hudson. "We'll go and stay at the Métropole; we might hear something there."

The Métropole proved to be an hotel of some importance—one of those hotels in which the manager makes a point of attending on distinguished visitors in the dining-room and engaging them in conversation. That these visitors were distinguished was shown by Mr. Hudson's choice from the wine list.

The manager advanced deferentially and asked whether the dinner was to their liking.

"Okay," said Mr. Hudson.

"Monsieur is Americain? I thought that you were English."

"Do you get many English here?"

"We used to, but now with the exchange, not so many. I regret it. My daughter was educated in England, and it is good for her not to forget what she learned."

Jim Milsom sat up and took notice. "Is she the young lady at the desk?" he asked.

"Yes, monsieur."

When he had withdrawn to other duties, Milsom said, "Now you'd better let this English-speaking daughter be my job. In looks she's quite passable. I shall get on with her like a house on fire. Shell tell me all about the mysterious Godfrey, and a good deal more, I fancy."

"Well," remarked Richardson, "it will fit in with my plans, for if Mr. Hudson doesn't mind, I thought of writing my report this evening in case I might forget something."

Mr. Hudson seemed to smile upon the project. His eye was a little glazed, and his whole attitude suggested that he would spend the evening profitably by dozing in the smoking-room with a long cigar dangling from his lips; he had fed well and sipped copiously.

Accordingly the party broke up to go its several ways. Richardson had retired to his bedroom to write, and had arrived at his fifth page when there was a sharp rap at the door, and Jim Milsom burst in, triumphant.

"I've had a spot of luck, Inspector. The young lady at the desk was dying to air her English. She learned it in a Catholic school in Jersey. It's the funniest kind of English that ever you heard, but quite pleasant to listen to. She said that she remembered your man Godfrey quite well, but I permitted myself to doubt her. Anyway, look what I've got for you— this letter. She said that it came just after Godfrey left, and as he hadn't left any address it's been lying waiting for him in the office ever since. Now, if you'd interviewed her, you'd have had qualms about accepting the letter, because you wouldn't have cared to say that you were one of Godfrey's intimate friends."

"On the contrary, Mr. Milsom, I should have gone further than you did, for I propose to open this letter and read it."

"Now you're talking. Let me see you do it."

"Oh, I haven't any of the gadgets that the postal censors used during the war. I have to do it as jealous wives do when they steal letters addressed to their husbands, in the hope of finding a woman's signature and an assignation." He went to the washstand, ran an inch of water into the basin, and laid the back of the letter to float on the surface without wetting the address. "There! In ten minutes it will be open without leaving a trace."

"May I wait? I won't interrupt your writing if you'll let me smoke."

"Sit down by all means. I shall have finished in a very few minutes."

For once in his life Jim Milsom maintained a silence that could be felt. He watched Richardson's pen traversing the page with what seemed to him incredible swiftness: the man never seemed to have to think what to say next. It was that faculty, he thought, that must have brought his friend such quick promotion—that and his habit of clearing up the smallest detail. A man like Richardson, he thought, would have succeeded in any walk of life, and here he was, content with the exiguous salary of detective inspector, because he loved his work for its own sake instead of pursuing it for what it would bring him in wealth and influence.

At last Richardson laid down his pen and went quickly to the washstand. He took out the letter, let the drops fall back into the basin, dabbed it with a towel, and tested the flap of the envelope with a little pocket paper-knife. Milsom rose and stood over him. Both the letter and the envelope were of cheap paper, and the handwriting was untutored. The letter was in French, but a French so simple that even Richardson could translate it. It read as follows:

> 21 RUE MARCECHAL FOCH,
> MELUN.
> 14 *Janvier*, 1934.

"SIR,

"Having read your advertisement in *Paris-Soir*, I hasten to inform you that my wife and I will be glad to accept the charge of the little English boy provided that the terms offered are sufficient. Awaiting your reply, I beg you to accept the assurance of my consideration the most distinguished.

"HENRI BIGOT."

The address on the envelope was M. Godfrey, Hotel Metropole, Orleans.

"Now we are getting on," cried Milsom. "All we have to do is round up this joker, Bignot, take him by the larynx, and make him produce the boy."

"No, Mr. Milsom. You forget that this letter has never been seen by this Mr. Godfrey, because he left this hotel two days before the letter came and left no address. But we do know from this that he advertised in the *Paris-Soir* between December 25th and January 14th for someone to take charge of a little boy. We need not trouble to go to the writer of this letter; all we have to do is to search the files of *Paris-Soir* between those dates. I dare say they take the paper in at this hotel."

"Right! Then that will be a job for Adolphe. Last Christmas Day and January 14th? I'll go and dig him out."

Five minutes later he returned triumphant with an armful of newspapers. "Adolphe had the devil's own luck. He's dug out the bally lot—all except one. Shall I go through them?"

"We'll do it together. Give me half of those papers. Now I suppose that the page to look at is the *Petites Annonces*. We'll try them first, looking for the name 'Godfrey.' I wonder why our friend chose a Paris paper."

"Adolphe tells me that it has an enormous circulation all over the country—mostly among the business people in little shops, and working people."

They worked on, unfolding each newspaper and scanning the advertisement column. Jim Milsom was the first to break the silence. "Here, what's this? Godfrey's name as large as life. Date—January 6th. Let me make a shot at the translation. It's under the column headed:

Offres de Places

Wanted, French family to take charge of English boy, aged 9. Liberal terms. Personal interview necessary. Address, M. Godfrey, Hôtel Métropole, Orleans.

How does that strike you?"

"May I look at it? Yes, sir, that's what we are in search of."

"Yes, Inspector, but how the devil are we going to find the other people who answered this advertisement. Are we to put in an advertisement of our own?—something like this: 'Will the gentleman who lately adopted a little English boy for a Mr. Godfrey, send his name and address to Mr. Richardson, Hotel Metropole, Orleans.'"

Richardson was lost in thought.

"You're not listening to me, Inspector."

"I beg your pardon. I'm afraid that I was thinking of something else." He took his note-case from his pocket and extracted from it a used postage-stamp with the postmark attached. "I wonder whether Mr. Hudson would mind driving us to Clermont-Ferrand next?"

"To Clermont-Ferrand? You're going to drop this case and go hunting the Bryants. Where is the damned place?"

"Right in the middle of France in what they call the Massif Central."

"Then it is the Bryants. I'm all for following up the case we came over for, but this new thing has taken hold of me."

"Don't worry, Mr. Milsom, I want to go to Clermont-Ferrand because I have what they call a hunch, a kind of intuition that we shall find the little boy there."

"Is that the famous postage-stamp?"

"Yes, the one I found treasured in Miss Clynes' room. I knew she had not been in France for many years and this postmark is dated only this year."

"The letter might have come to her from Bryant."

"No, because if the letter had been addressed to her she would have kept the envelope and not only the stamp and the postmark. She did not collect postage-stamps."

"I begin to see your idea. You think that Miss Clynes may have got wind of the little boy being alive. By Jove! Inspector, that opens up all sorts of possibilities. I believe you've hit it. And when you get to Clermont-Ferrand—I suppose it's a biggish place—how do you propose to proceed?"

"In the last resort we could advertise in the local paper, but I think the better way would be for me to go to the local Sûreté introduce myself as a colleague from Scotland Yard and get them to interest themselves. There must be quite a number of people who know that an English boy has been adopted by someone in the town. It may all come to nothing and turn out to be a waste of time, but as we are in France I think we should leave no stone unturned."

"Oh, you needn't worry about my uncle. Whatever you suggest to him goes. In your hands he's like an infant in a kindergarten. You can take it from me that we'll start to-morrow morning at eight o'clock."

Chapter Fifteen

ADOLPHE BROUGHT the car round, spick and span, at five minutes to eight and ran upstairs for his passengers' baggage. He found his employer in low spirits, which was always his wont in the early morning when coffee had to be swallowed at half-past seven.

"This is a ghastly hour to be starting, Adolphe. How far are we to go?"

"About two hundred and forty kilometres, sir—not a very long run."

"And we average sixty an hour with this car. Why, it's only a four hours' run. Why should we have to get away so early?"

"It was Mr. Milsom's order, sir. I fancy that he and the inspector hope to find out something important at Clermont during the afternoon."

"Oh, if that's the case I've nothing to say. Let's get on with it. Here's my grip-sack."

During the four hours' drive it became evident to Mr. Hudson's companions that he was making heroic efforts to restrain his curiosity. At last he made a timid move towards drawing Richardson out. "I don't know why we're going to this place, Clermont-Ferrand, but it's not for the beauty of the scenery, I guess, Inspector. You two boys got at something last night?"

Milsom squeezed Richardson's knee, but Richardson was too grateful to his benefactor to take the hint and join his nephew in what he called "guying" him. "Yes, Mr. Hudson, we found a letter and an advertisement in a French newspaper which showed that this Mr. Godfrey—the man we are following—was advertising for people to come forward and provide a home for a young English boy, no doubt the boy he had taken to three separate clinics. But I must warn you that this journey to Clermont-Ferrand may turn out to be a sheer waste of time and money."

"I don't mind that so long as we get at something in the end, and I've seen enough of your methods of working, Inspector, to feel sure now that we shall."

"I ought to warn you, sir, that we are going to Clermont-Ferrand on nothing stronger than a postage-stamp and a postmark which I found among the trinkets of that poor dead woman in London. Here they are."

Mr. Hudson adjusted his glasses and pored over the postage-stamp. "Waal, if this leads to anything I shall tell the world that you are its greatest sleuth! To get a murderer on a postage-stamp—why, it's just wonderful." He rubbed his fat hands together with the anticipation of a schoolboy.

"Don't build too much upon it, Mr. Hudson. In every difficult case there are a dozen false clues which end in a dead wall, but the point is that one can't afford to neglect any of them."

But Hudson had so touching a confidence in his fellow-traveller's *flair* that he refused to be discouraged. In his imagination the boy had already been found. "We'll put the little fella between us here on the back seat," he muttered, shifting himself into the corner to make room. "Gee! But he'll have a lot to tell us."

As the morning went on all became hungry. They passed through many towns and villages, but Adolphe ignored all the placards restricting the speed of cars to ten kilometres an hour and tore through them all. Once indeed Milsom ventured to call his uncle's attention to a promising-looking restaurant by the wayside, and suggested a halt for lunch, but the old man shook his head. "We'll get lunch at this place with the double name," he said; "we've gotta push on."

And now they began the long ascent to the central massif on the crest of which lay Clermont-Ferrand. The car took it in its stride without changing speed, even at the sharp turns of the road, without any perceptible anxiety in the features of its owner. When Adolphe shaved a two-horse hay-wagon which was imprudently taking the middle of the road and a wisp of hay was scraped off through the open window on to their knees, Milsom observed to the roof of the car, "I wonder what my Uncle James would have said if that had happened when I was at the wheel," but Mr. Hudson took no notice. The demon of speed had him in its grip. "We've gotta get on."

And now they were approaching the town. Adolphe turned in his seat to ask where they would stop for lunch.

"Any place," shouted his employer.

As Richardson expected, Adolphe took this to be an intimation that he was free to choose the best hotel in the place, and he pulled up at the Grand where the meals cost thirty-five francs and the garage ten.

So keen was Mr. Hudson on the quest of the postage-stamp that his nephew declared that he would have skipped his lunch if Adolphe had not assured him that nothing could be done in French towns during the hours sacred to the midday meal.

During lunch Richardson broke it to his hosts that he must visit the local office of the Sûreté Générate alone, with Adolphe as his interpreter. "You see, sir," he explained to Mr. Hudson, "I shall have to introduce myself as a police colleague from London, and if there are four of us the police commissaire may take you for journalists and shut up like an oyster, but there is no reason why you should not wait outside in the car. Besides, it may all lead to nothing."

"Is that so?" commented Mr. Hudson dryly. "I guess that you'll come out waving an address in our faces; Adolphe will drive us to the house and you'll come out leading a little English boy by the hand."

Milsom pronounced half-past one to be the magic hour when French officials might be trusted to receive inquisitive foreigners with a tolerant eye. "Besides, their men, who have to go off on cycles to make their inquiries, will be found in the office, full-fed and at peace with the world."

Armed with the address and a plan of the town, Adolphe drove them straight to the door of the commissariat, and he and Richardson went in and asked the Sûreté officer in the outer room to take Richardson's card to his chief. "You might tell him that I have come straight from Scotland Yard, the head-quarters of the London police, to ask for the aid of the Sûreté in bringing a murderer to justice," added Richardson. The officer returned and beckoned to the two to follow him.

They found themselves in a little room in which the floor space was restricted by cupboards and a large writing-table encumbered with papers. The officer at the table rose and came forward to shake hands with Richardson as a colleague. He brought two chairs up to the table for his guests and asked what he could do for them.

"You do not speak French, monsieur? You have brought your chauffeur to interpret for you?"

Richardson assented, regretting more than ever that he lacked the linguistic accomplishments of his colleagues in the Special Branch. Adolphe interpreted what he said, sentence by sentence.

"The President of Police in London has sent me out to France in connection with the murder of a lady in London, monsieur, and one branch of the inquiry concerns an English boy who was injured in the accident at Lagny on Christmas Eve. There is some reason for believing that he may be in Clermont-Ferrand."

"What was his age?"

"About nine."

"Then he cannot be alone here."

"No, monsieur. If he is here he must be in some French family. This advertisement that appeared in the *Paris-Soir* of January 6th produced this reply from a Frenchman living in a different part of the country, but the advertiser had already left his hotel when this letter arrived for him."

"You think that he may have had another reply from Clermont-Ferrand?"

"Yes, monsieur, that is why we are here."

The officer pursed his lips doubtfully. "Sit still, gentlemen, while I make inquiries of my subordinates whether any of them have heard of an English boy being in the town."

In less than five minutes he returned with a young, smart-looking police officer in breeches and gaiters, who was about to start off on his bicycle.

"Happily, messieurs, I was just in time. This officer was already on his bicycle when I stopped him. He will be able to tell you something of interest. Speak, Commissaire Bigot."

Bigot stood to attention while he rattled off his report. "A bicycle repairer in rue de Serbie has an English boy living with him. One day I stopped to inquire how he came by him. He told me that an English milord had advertised for a family to take charge of the boy and he replied to the advertisement; that the English milord brought the boy in a large touring car, but the boy was ill and the man hesitated to accept him in that condition. The boy had bandage round his head. A month later I was passing the shop and I stopped to ask whether the boy had recovered, whether he had an identity card, and whether he was attending school. While I was putting these questions the boy himself ran out of the workshop. Already he could speak a few words of French."

"Would you allow this officer to guide us to the shop?" asked Richardson.

"Certainly; he can go ahead on his bicycle and your car can follow him. Do you propose to leave the boy here or to take him back with you?"

"Probably we shall take him back to England if his evidence proves to be of any value, monsieur."

Richardson took his leave with the feeling that fortune was smiling on him and with warm appreciation of the efficiency of the Sûreté Générate.

"Well, what luck?" asked Milsom, when he returned to the car; "and who's this brigand armed to the teeth on a bicycle?"

"Hush, Mr. Milsom; he may understand English. He's to act as our guide."

"What's that?" inquired his uncle. "You mean to say that we've found that boy?"

"I hope, sir, that you will be talking to him in five minutes."

The "brigand" in blue breeches mounted his cycle and Adolphe followed him, towards the north-west part of the town. He rode fast and made a signal to Adolphe at each corner. They came soon to a tramway crossing and a narrow ill-paved street. This was the rue de Serbie. The officer slowed down, holding up his hand to Adolphe, swung his leg over the saddle of his machine and entered the door of the little two-storeyed cycle shop. Richardson and Adolphe were close upon his heels. The cycle repairer, an alert little man with grubby hands, came forward to meet them.

"Where's that English boy?" asked the commissaire.

"He's at school, monsieur. He won't be back until after five. Which school? Why, the school in the Avenue des États Unis."

"I want you to tell these gentlemen how the boy came to you. It is the Brigadier's orders that you tell them everything. And now, messieurs, if you will excuse me, I will leave you and attend to my other duties. You will no doubt report to my Brigadier what steps you have taken as regards the boy." He saluted and rode away on his bicycle.

The little cycle-repairer scratched his head. "Did I do wrong in accepting the boy, monsieur? I read the advertisement and talked things over with my wife. With your leave I will call her. She knows more about the little boy than I do." He stamped on the lowest step of the staircase and shouted, "Louise."

"*J'arrive*," came the reply from the upper regions.

"You see, messieurs, we have no children of our own and you know what women are—always they want children." Louise, a buxom lass in the early twenties, made her appearance and stood smiling at her husband's side.

"You are talking about little Jean. He is getting on well now, but of course at first he was lonely. He could not speak our language, poor boy, and no one could understand him, but now he is beginning and he has boys to play with at school."

"After you replied to the advertisement what happened?" asked Richardson.

"Two days later a big car drove up to the door and a milord, who spoke French very well, lifted the little boy out of the car and carried him into this workshop. Louise insisted on taking him into her kitchen where it was clean and there were chairs to sit on. There the Englishman told us the little boy's story. His father had been condemned in England and was in prison; that they did not want little Jean ever to know of this and so they brought him to France to be brought up as a French child. I do not hide the truth from you, monsieur, the gentleman made us a very generous offer—an offer that will enable me to move into a larger workshop and engage hands to extend my business. It was a great temptation to a poor mechanic like myself. I told him that I would accept the charge of the boy and adopt him as my son, but that it would be necessary for us both to sign an agreement as regards the adoption and have it certified at the Mairie. If you will wait a moment I will go and fetch my copy of the agreement."

While he was gone, Richardson asked his wife whether she had grown fond of the boy.

"It was difficult at first, monsieur. The poor child was ailing, and we could not understand each other's language. He seemed to be suffering with his head. He talked in his sleep a great deal. He must have had terrible dreams, poor child, but gradually he got better. Since he has been at school and mixing with other children he has made great progress in French."

The husband returned with the deed of adoption. Adolphe ran his eye over it. "This must have been drafted by a lawyer," he said.

"Yes," replied the husband; "it was drafted by Maître Delage in the Avenue Maréchal Joffre, and as you see we both signed it before the mayor. You will observe the stamp of the Maine."

Adolphe handed it back to him and Richardson asked, "Can I see the little boy?"

The man turned to his wife. "Run up to the school, Louise, and tell them that some English people are passing through the town and desire to see Jean. Bring him back with you."

The woman trotted off without a hat, and Richardson turned to Adolphe. "I'm going off to consult my friends in the car. While I'm gone will you find out from the husband whether he and his wife would mind very much if we took the boy away with us?"

He went out to the car and found its owner beaming with anticipation.

"You've found the boy, then?"

"Yes, Mr. Hudson; he's at school at the moment, but his foster-mother has gone off to fetch him. I find myself in some difficulty because I'm not conversant with French law. These people were told that the boy's father was in prison, and they have legally adopted this little boy as their son; and I can't represent myself to them as an English relative who wants to take the boy away from them, I might be committing an offence against French law."

"Don't ask me about French law and French lawyers. I'm a property owner in the country, and I hate the very sight of them."

Jim Milsom broke in. "Look here, Inspector, don't waste time by splitting straws. Leave it to me. I'll kidnap the boy and have done with it. What I don't know about kidnapping isn't worth knowing."

"No doubt, Mr. Milsom, but then we should have sensational paragraphs in the French newspapers, and perhaps questions in the House of Commons, and I might find myself in serious trouble."

"Well, then, a little lying wouldn't come amiss. You, of course, as a public official must tell nothing but the truth, but I'm free as a fiction editor to tell them anything that'll go. I'll say that the boy's father isn't in prison; that on the contrary he's in heaven, and that the guy who brought him here had no rights over him—that he stole him, in fact; that you are his nearest relative, his paternal uncle, and you want him back."

"And you might add," said Mr. Hudson, "that if a small sum of money would be of any use to them...If I was in your place, Inspector, I should just tell them who I was—an inspector from Scotland Yard. I should say, 'See here, now, Scotland Yard has sent me to bring that boy back to England, and no guy in blue breeches is going to stop me doing it.' And if they grumbled a bit I should say, 'If it's a bit of money you want, I'll pay you a bit of compensation if you don't open your mouths too wide.'"

Adolphe approached them at a quick walk and addressed Richardson. "It's all right, Inspector. The missus is fond of the boy, but the doctor has given her a bit of good news. She's expecting—is that what you say in English? When they wanted to adopt a child it was because they thought she couldn't have one of her own."

"Well, then, everything's okay," said Mr. Hudson. "I'm eager to see that little fellow and hear what he has to tell us."

Adolphe was looking up the road. "They're coming, sir."

The three jumped out of the ear and stood waiting. They saw Louise pointing at them. The little boy broke from her and came running towards them. In spite of his deplorable French clothing, he was manifestly an English boy.

"Maman tells me you are English. Are you really English?" His candid blue eyes looked from one to the other.

"I should jolly well think we are," said Jim Milsom, who had a way with little boys. "What's your name, old man?"

"Well, here they call me Jean Godfrey, but Godfrey's my first name. My real name is Godfrey Maze."

Chapter Sixteen

LOUISE, WITH the hospitable instinct of the French peasant, insisted that they all go into her kitchen and taste her coffee. There were to be no refusals. Chairs were fetched from other rooms until there were sufficient for all. The hostess busied herself about her kitchen range: Jim Milsom put his arm round little Godfrey Maze and asked him how he would like to go with them to England.

The boy's eyes blazed with excitement. "Wouldn't I just! But what will Maman say?"

"Oh, we're going to make it all right with Maman. Don't you worry."

Meanwhile, Richardson suggested to Adolphe that while the coffee was being made they should take the adopted father into his workshop and have a talk with him. The three left the room together.

"Tell him," said Richardson, "that the gentleman who brought the boy here had no right to sign that deed of adoption; that he lied when he told him that that boy's father was in prison—that, in fact, the father is dead and the boy is heir to a considerable fortune in England. All this can easily be proved in a French court, but that would cost time and money, and there would be publicity in the newspapers which we are anxious to avoid. Ask him whether he would object to the boy leaving with us, and consider the deed of adoption as null and void?"

Adolphe translated all this to the astonished mechanic.

"Messieurs," he replied, "my wife has grown attached to that boy, but we have both realized that he is not happy with us; that he is not of our class. We ought, of course, to let him go back to his own folks, but it is a question of the money we have had. Happily it has not yet been spent, but I have been in treaty for new premises, and they may hold me to pay the law expenses."

"Tell him that there is no question of asking him to refund any of the money. All that is required is that he should tear up that deed of adoption and allow us to take the child away."

There was intense relief in the man's features when he heard the statement about the money, but Richardson detected an expression of fear when he understood that he was being asked to tear up a document with an official seal on it. "But suppose, messieurs, that the Maire requires me to produce this document. He may say, 'What proof had you that the gentleman who called upon you had more right to the boy than the gentleman who signed that deed?'"

There was no answer to that question. Not one of them had a better claim to the boy than his guardian, John Maze.

"Tell him, then, that he can keep the document to produce if he is required to do so, but that the child must come back with us to England, as he is required to give evidence against the man who signed that document in a false name, and to enable him to claim the property that was left to him by his father."

"You mean that little Jean has inherited property, messieurs?" He spoke in a tone of new respect for his adopted son.

"Yes, a very considerable property, we believe, and the boy's evidence will be required to enable him to claim it."

"I am content, messieurs, to let him go. I will tell my wife to pack his valise. And now I hear her calling us. The coffee and the *goûter* must be ready."

In spite of the approaching parting, it was a gay little meal. Jim Milsom's sallies kept little Godfrey in gurgles of laughter: Louise herself found it infectious as she pressed biscuits and coffee on her guests. When all except the little boy showed that they could eat and drink no more, the cycle-mechanic signalled to his wife and they left the room together. Mr. Hudson seized the opportunity for a whispered colloquy with Richardson.

"Say, Inspector, I would like to stand in on this. If a wad of notes would soften the blow for these poor folks, why, they ought to have it, see? You might slip it to them without telling them where it came from."

"It's very good of you, Mr. Hudson, but you've done too much for us already. I don't think that the man wants any more money. His fear was that we should ask him to refund some of what he's already got, and also that he might get into trouble with the French authorities if he allowed me to destroy that deed. As for the wife, I think that she is genuinely fond of the little boy and will miss him until she has a child. What would really please her would be a photograph of the little boy taken with her—a photograph that she could show to her friends in after years."

"I thought that these French peasants were always after money."

"Of course you know more about them than I do, Mr. Hudson, but if I can judge at all what is passing through a man's mind, I should say that a sort of sturdy pride was uppermost in that man's mind, and that to offer him more money would wound it. I believe that he would refuse to take it."

"That's okay then, Inspector. We'll take the woman along in the car, and the man, too, if he'd like to come, drive to the best photographer in the town, and get a framed portrait done of the three of them. I wouldn't have missed this show for all the world."

The foster-father and mother came down from the bedroom carrying a cheap little suitcase. There were tears in the woman's eyes. Adolphe was called in to interpret. Mr. Hudson spoke.

"Tell them that we are all going down to the photographer to have a picture done of them with the little boy, and that some day, when he's a grown man, he will come out in a car of his own to visit them."

The woman clasped her hands in delight. She ran to the child and kissed him. "Thou hearest, Jean? We are all going to be photographed, and I shall have thy portrait always to look at when thou art far away!"

The man flew to his workshop to wash his hands and face, comb his hair and put on a coat. Somehow the party was packed into the car, and Adolphe was bidden to find the best photographer in the town. Guided by the cycle-man, he pulled up at a mean-looking little photographer's shop in the next street, but this did not suit Mr. Hudson.

"Drive back to the Grand Hotel," he commanded.

"They'll tell us where to find the best man in the town."

A few minutes later, when they had been directed to the smartest photographer in the town, and the little couple saw where they had pulled up, they were covered with confusion. Richardson could read in Louise's face dismay at the thought that she was not wearing her best Sunday frock. The party filled the little shop decorated with specimens of the master's art—principally wedding groups of the local bourgeoisie.

Adolphe interpreted to the astonished photographer the desires of his employer. "It is to be a large picture—a sort of exhibition picture—in the handsomest gilt frame you have----"

The artist pointed mutely to his *chef-d'oeuvres* displayed on the walls.

"No, it's got to be bigger than any of these. Now get on with it."

The couple and little Godfrey Maze were conducted to the studio upstairs and were left to the whim of the artist. In five minutes they came clattering down. Godfrey ran to Jim Milsom. "He took us four times, Uncle Jim! And he made us change where we looked at each time. He lifted up my face by my chin," he added with awe.

The photographer came in to complete the business arrangements with his eccentric customers. The price was agreed to without demur—another eccentricity—the money was paid over; addresses were exchanged; an unframed copy of each photograph was to be sent to Jim Milsom in London, and the framed copy of the best was to be sent to the cycle-shop.

"There is one thing that we ought to do, Mr. Hudson, while we have the cycle-man with us. We ought to go to the lawyer who drew up that agreement of adoption which is registered in the Mairie, and ask him whether any legal formalities will be required for cancelling it. A complication may arise from the fact that only one of the parties to the agreement is present, but a French lawyer can generally discover some loophole, and his fee cannot be very large."

"You needn't worry about the fee. That's my share of the joy-ride. Adolphe, ask that gentleman beside you to show you the way to the lawyer who drew up that agreement."

From the little man's excited gestures they gathered that it was quite near.

Maître Delage lived on the first floor of a house at least three centuries old. He was a hirsute personage, and between his beard and his spectacles there was little to be seen of his face. Adolphe introduced the party as a distinguished company of English noble-men, who had come on a mission to France to take back with them a young nobleman who had been legally confided to the care of Louise and her husband by mistake. Adolphe felt in his heart that it would cost his employer double the ordinary fee, but that he would submit to the extortion with a glad heart.

The bearded *maître* scanned the agreement and nodded his beard over it three times. "Where is the gentleman who signed this agreement? It cannot be abrogated by one party without the other."

"Tell him," murmured Richardson, "that the gentleman in question is a criminal; and that he signed the agreement under a false name."

"Then he has committed a crime in this country, and your course is clear. If you can prove that the name he signed was false, you can have him arrested. The agreement, at any rate, is void."

He emphasized his verdict by thumping the table with a fat hand.

They trooped out to the car: the parting was to take place on the pavement. Richardson found himself wondering whether with all this excitement the boy would submit properly to the caresses of his foster-parents, since boys are apt to be callous under such circumstances. He need not have been anxious. Louise was sobbing quietly to herself as she folded him in her arms: the boy hugged and kissed her with real and unaffected warmth: there were tears in his eyes as she gently disengaged herself. The man insisted on kissing him, too, in the French fashion, and he responded no less warmly.

It was now nearly five o'clock, and there was still one formality to be complied with before they left the town. Richardson asked to be driven back to the Gendarmerie station to report to the Brigadier, and to thank him for what he had done for them.

"You are taking the boy back with you to England, monsieur?"

"Yes. monsieur. His evidence is likely to be very important in the case I mentioned to you. I shall not fail to report to my *préfet* the great service you have rendered to the cause of justice."

The man purred with satisfaction as they shook hands.

The question now arose where they were to pass the night. "Paris is only just over three hundred and eighty kilometres from here," observed Adolphe.

"We could get in by half-past ten," said Milsom, who was dying to get on.

"We could—if we didn't stop to dine," retorted his uncle, who was old enough to remember his creature-comforts. "Where could we stop on the way to dine and sleep?"

"Bourges is on the way, sir. There's a good hotel there."

"Okay! We'll stop at Bourges and send that boy to bed early. He'll have done enough for one day."

This last reflection was borne out half an hour later, when Godfrey careened over towards Richardson and fell fast asleep. His elders, also, were growing somnolent, and soon silence fell upon the car.

It was not until two hours later, when they were nearing Bourges, that Jim Milsom sprang into wakefulness. "Well, I'm damned!" he exclaimed. "Inspector Richardson asleep on duty! I ought to report this at the Yard."

Richardson opened his eyes and smiled. "When one has a serious problem to unravel, Mr. Milsom, one always does it better with the eyes closed."

Little Godfrey rubbed his eyes, sat bolt upright, and stared out of the window.

"You've been dreaming, young man, haven't you?"

"Yes, I've been dreaming about Uncle John."

"What do you remember about him?" asked Richardson.

"Well, not very much. I remember being in his big house in Liverpool, and his butler, Reynolds, who made me an aeroplane out of bottle-corks and wire. I remember being in a steamer with him, but I didn't enjoy it because I was sick. But I don't know how I got to Clermont-Ferrand. I don't remember going there. I know that Maman told me that I'd been ill."

"When you got better what did you do?"

"How do you mean, what did I do? The first thing I did was to write a letter to my uncle. Maman bought the stamp when she went out to market and posted the letter for me, but Uncle John never answered it. P'r'aps I ought to have written to Miss Bates."

"Was Miss Bates your governess?"

"Yes, it was Miss Bates who taught me to write."

"What did you say in your letter?"

"Oh, I told Uncle John that I didn't like Clermont-Ferrand, and that I wanted to get back to Liverpool. But he never answered it, and when I asked Maman to buy another stamp for me to write to Miss Bates, she said that Papa had told her that I mustn't write any letters to England."

"Why didn't you like Clermont-Ferrand?" asked Jim Milsom.

"Because I couldn't make anyone understand me at first. Maman always understood me and taught me how to say things in French. I liked Maman and Papa, but not Clermont-Ferrand."

"Huh!" grunted Mr. Hudson; "that stamp's accounted for then."

They were now running through a street; they were on the outskirts of the town. Adolphe slowed down a little later and brought the car to a standstill before the Hotel d'Angleterre, where English of a kind was spoken. Mr. Hudson went to the desk to engage the rooms: little Godfrey was to have a room all to himself, and, moreover, he was to have late dinner with the others. It was quite a lively dinner, for Jim Milsom, whom little Godfrey persisted in calling "Uncle Jim," kept the ball rolling.

"You know that we shall be in Paris to-morrow, Godfrey?"

The name seemed to convey nothing to the boy.

"In Paris! Where's that?"

"It's the capital of France."

"Oh, I thought Clermont-Ferrand was. Is Paris bigger than Clermont-Ferrand?"

"Much bigger; and shall I tell you what I'm going to do as soon as we get there? I'm going to take you to a tailor for some new clothes. You couldn't go about Paris in clothes like that."

"Why? Don't you like this ribbon at my neck? Maman was telling me how to tie it myself. I told her that boys never wore bows like that in England— that only little girls wore them—but she wouldn't listen."

"I'm going to get you a tie like mine and a proper kind of collar, and dress you exactly like an English schoolboy. You'll like that, won't you?"

"Yes, I shall."

Mr. Hudson broke in." And while you're away at the tailor's I'm going to do a little shopping. I'm going to get you a proper leather suitcase and then I know a shop where they sell all kinds of things."

"Do you propose to stay in Paris, sir?" asked Richardson anxiously. "I ask only because I feel that I ought to be getting back to London as soon as possible. In a case of this kind there is never any time to lose. You see, something might appear in a local paper in Clermont. Mr. Maze might get wind of it and clear out. Besides, sir, if you're thinking of buying things for the boy that he won't be wearing on the journey, there's the British customs to think of. If I might suggest you would be doing better by buying them in London."

"You're right again, Inspector. The toys there would be better and cheaper than in Paris."

"Now, young man, it's time for bed," declared Jim Milsom. "I suppose you know how to put yourself to bed."

"Of course I do, Uncle Jim."

"Then come along and I'll show you your room." When Jim Milsom rejoined his companions he found Richardson in deep conversation with Mr. Hudson. "As I was saying, sir, there's no secret about the position. When John Maze brought his nephew over to France he had no thought of any foul play. I fancy that he wanted to be rid of the boy because as an old bachelor he found his nephew a nuisance in the house. It was only when he saw the bodies of those unclaimed children after the accident that he conceived the idea of substituting one of them for his nephew."

"What was the motive for that?"

"I think that we shall find that there was a very sufficient motive, but now please understand that I'm speaking from conjecture. This little boy is the only son of Mr. Maze's elder brother, and presumably the elder brother's property was left to his son. If the death of the son could be proved, I imagine that this property would go to John Maze as his next of kin. It'll be quite easy to ascertain whether this conjecture is correct as soon as I get to London."

"Gee! Fate played into that guy's hands. First the boy gets a knock on the head and loses his memory. Second he takes him to three different clinics on plausible excuses and gets three different medical opinions about the loss of memory. Then he advertises and finds that couple to adopt the child right away in the middle of France where no one ever goes."

"Yes, sir, it must have been a severe shock to Mr. Maze when he got that letter from the boy."

"Yes, but nothing like the shock that's coming to him when you get back. Now, I gather that you want to get over to-morrow."

"I feel I ought to, sir."

"Well, we can't get you to Paris in time for the morning train by Dieppe, nor for Imperial Airways."

"Look here, Inspector," said Milsom. "Please understand that I decline to be seen travelling with a nephew in fancy dress. You must give me time to buy a pair of reach-me-downs such as are worn by Christians. That means that we shall stay to-morrow and to-morrow night in Paris."

"Would you mind very much, sir, if I went on ahead by the night train to-morrow? I should be in London at six next morning and that would give me the whole day for my inquiries."

"Not a bit. You will find us all at my flat in the evening if you care to come round."

"Very good, sir, that's settled." A sudden alarm showed in his eyes. "I hope that we can count upon you, Mr. Milsom, not to do anything rash."

"Rash! What do you take me for?"

"I mean that I can count upon you to have the boy always where I can find him if he's wanted. You see, there'll be a lot of legal business to go through and the proof of his evidence to be taken if it's wanted."

"You think I'm going to spirit him away. By Jove! That's an idea. I'd rather like to see what it feels like to be the hare with you after me as the hound. I'd lead you a dance, Inspector."

"I've no doubt you would, sir, and I sincerely hope that you won't. Of course I know that you're joking and that you're as keen as I am to get to the bottom of this case."

"You needn't be scared, Inspector," said Mr. Hudson, "I shall make myself responsible for the boy, and you know when the time comes I shall apply to your people for leave to adopt him as a son or a nephew or something."

"A nephew, Uncle Jim? You've got me."

"Well, I've had a failure with one nephew and I should like to see what I can make of this little fellow."

"You haven't forgotten, sir," said Richardson, "that we shall probably find that the boy is heir to a big fortune."

"Well, if he is, I can look after him all the same: I don't want his money."

"Now, you folks, what about bed if we've got to make an early start?" said Milsom, yawning. "And what about ordering breakfast at eight?—that will get us into Paris by lunch-time."

The next morning when Jim Milsom went to wake his new-found nephew, he found him already out of bed and half dressed. He looked the picture of health.

"Why, you're not dressed, Uncle Jim; you'll be late for breakfast."

"What time do you breakfast in Clermont-Ferrand?"

"At seven o'clock, of course."

"My God!" ejaculated Jim under his breath.

"Now, young man, do you feel up to a busy day in Paris?"

"I feel up to anything."

"Good, then finish your dressing and I'll tell the waiter to bring my breakfast and yours together and put it on that table."

Godfrey clapped his hands in ecstasy. "I'm awfully glad I found you, Uncle Jim; or was it you who found me?"

"A little of both—about half and half, I think, but you get on with your dressing and I'll get on with mine."

An hour later they were well on the road to Paris. After lunching at the Crillon, Jim Milsom carried Godfrey off on a mysterious excursion while Richardson retired to the writing-room to arrange his notes and complete his report. It was arranged that the party should dine early and see Richardson off at the Gare St. Lazare.

The dinner-hour drew on when suddenly a small boy burst into the writing-room alone and ran to Richardson's table. He had had his hair cut; he was clad correctly in grey flannels with a collar and a sports tie. For the moment Richardson could not place him until the youngster addressed him.

"What do you think of my new clothes?"

Having duly admired them, Richardson conducted him to the dining-room where the other two members of the party had sat down.

"When we've seen you off at the station, Inspector," said Milsom. "I'm going to carry this young man off to see a show."

"You young scoundrel," exclaimed the scandalized uncle, "fancy taking a boy of nine to see a show in Paris."

"Ah, ah!" exclaimed Jim; "I'd always suspected it. When you're in Paris you go to the *Folies Bergère*. I'm going to take Godfrey to the pictures at the Paramount. What have you to say against that?"

Richardson felt that in spite of his habitual banter Jim Milsom could be trusted to keep his word and have the boy at his flat on the evening of their arrival.

Chapter Seventeen

A MAN does not feel at his best when he arrives in London at 6 a.m. on a wet morning after a stormy night crossing. But Inspector Richardson had the gift of subordinating every discomfort to the business he had in hand. There was no time, he thought, to go out to his lodgings in Forest Gate and get back in time for the hour when the public is admitted to Somerset House. He had a scratch breakfast at Victoria, and a wash and a shave at a shop outside the station. Then, having deposited his luggage in the cloakroom, he made his way to Scotland Yard and sought out Sergeant Williams.

"Back already, Inspector! You have still three days' leave to take."

"I know, but I've got on to something good that cannot wait. That's why I'm back. What have you been doing while I've been away?"

"I've quite a lot to tell you. You remember that man, Wilfred Bryant? Well, he was here on Tuesday asking for you, and I saw him."

"What did he want?"

"He'd come to tell you that he remembered something that would prove an alibi for the night of the murder. He had gone, as he told us, into Lyons' shop in Piccadilly to get a bite of supper, but he said that what he forgot to tell us was an incident that he had there with the waitress. When he paid for his meal he handed her one of those new French ten-franc pieces in mistake for a florin. She took it to the desk where the cashier declined to accept it, so back she came to him to put the matter right. He gave her a florin and told her that she could keep the French coin as a souvenir. That's the kind of thing that a Lyons' waitress wouldn't forget. I went round there and dug the girl out. She'd let her tongue run on, for every waitress in the place had heard the story, and said it was Betty. The young lady was summoned, and I took a statement from her. Here it is. It confirms exactly what Bryant told me. Now, I suppose, we shall have to start this blooming case right from the beginning again."

"No, we shan't. I've come back from France with the goods."

"What do you mean?"

"I know now who the real murderer was, and if all goes well this morning, he'll be under lock and key to-morrow."

By the time he had finished telling Williams the story, the clock marked the hour when the public is admitted to Somerset House. Like other Metropolitan detectives, he knew his way about Somerset House. He had to establish the family history of the Mazes of Liverpool. After finding an obliging clerk whom he knew, the quest became easy. He was allowed to take a copy of the will of Godfrey Maze, the founder of the family fortunes, who left the comfortable sum of £182,000 when he departed to another and a better world. The bulk of this property had gone to his elder son, William, and his heirs; failing any heirs to the elder brother, the property was to go to John and his heirs.

Further researches established the fact that William Maze had been twice married; that his first wife had died childless when he was fifty-five; that at the age of fifty-seven he had married again, and his wife had borne him a son, dying in childbirth. This son was named Godfrey, after his grandfather.

William had died in October, 1933, leaving his son to the guardianship of his brother John, who was trustee for the boy's property. If the boy were to die, the whole of the property would go, under the terms of the grandfather's will, to John Maze absolutely.

Richardson's heart gave a bound when he made this discovery. He now began to put two and two together. During little Godfrey's prattlings on the journey to Paris, he had gathered that the uncle, John Maze, did not care for small boys, and was easily put out by the noise and the mess they made about a house; that he had also said that a big boy of nine was too much for a governess; that he ought to be at some foreign school where he could learn languages. The whole story seemed now to be unfolded.

Obviously his next business would be to report the results of his inquiries to Mr. Morden, his Chief, and take instructions as to how he should proceed.

He was received with some astonishment by the colleagues he met in the passage. "I thought you were on leave," said Inspector Graves. "We didn't expect you back for another three days. Couldn't you keep away from the place?

Richardson replied in the same bantering vein. "I've been motoring in France and I couldn't stand the food any longer."

"Go on! Motoring in France, indeed!"

"Is Mr. Morden in the office?"

Graves glanced at the clock. "Oh, he's there all right, but he'll bite your head off if you go and see him now. He's just come from a conference at the Home Office—a full dress affair over that Randall case, and his table's piled high with stuff he's to get through by lunch-time."

"I can't help it; my case is more pressing than anything else he's got on his table; so here goes."

Somewhat to Richardson's surprise the messenger returned from Morden and nodded to him. He went in. His Chief was almost hidden by the rampart of police files built round him.

"What's brought you back from leave, Mr. Richardson?"

"I think I've solved that murder case in Chelsea, sir."

"The devil you have! I was talking about it to Sir William only yesterday. Where have you been while you were on leave?"

"In France, sir."

"Taking a busman's holiday; oh, yes, I remember. You can't keep off your work even for a week. Weren't you following up that man Bryant and his wife?"

"Yes, sir, I was, but while doing so I ran into a chain of evidence that cleared Bryant and fixed the guilt on another man altogether."

"Well, who is he?"

"Mr. John Maze, a retired solicitor in Liverpool."

Morden wrinkled his brow in thought. "You don't mean the murdered woman's former employer?"

"Yes, sir; he had a strong motive for the crime, and he has committed another crime on which he can be arrested. He has sworn a false affidavit that his nephew was killed in that accident at Lagny, near Paris, with the object of possessing himself of the boy's property."

"How do you know that?"

"I've read the affidavit at Somerset House this morning, sir; and I've brought the boy back with me from France alive."

"Good God! You don't do things by halves. Tell me the whole story."

Richardson had acquired the knack of relating the story of a crime concisely, without missing any material point.

When he had finished his Chief remarked, "I see that you have a watertight case as regards the false affidavit. I suppose that the connecting link between that and the murder in Chelsea is the postage-stamp with the Clermont-Ferrand postmark?"

"Yes, sir, and I ought to add that the little boy told me that he knew Miss Clynes; that his uncle had once taken him down to his office and had left him with her, and that she had allowed him to tap on her typewriter. He even remembered her name."

"Do you mean that he wrote to her—that that postmark you found in her jewel-case had been torn off an envelope addressed to her?"

"No, sir; I think that the postmark came from a letter which the little boy had written to his uncle, that she retrieved the envelope from the wastepaper basket."

"I see; so Maze regarded her as a dangerous person —the only person in the world who had guessed his secret. What do you propose to do now?"

"With your approval, sir, I should like to run up to Liverpool and take Maze into custody. His offence of swearing a false affidavit is a felony: he can be arrested without a warrant, and his house can be searched: also, we can take his fingerprints and compare them with the print found on the spacing-bar of the murdered woman's typewriter."

"True, but I think that you had better swear an information at Bow Street, and get a warrant for his arrest, which you can take to the Chief Constable of Liverpool for execution. You can take a letter from us asking, as a matter of form, that you be allowed to accompany the officers who execute the warrant."

"Very good, sir. I'll get the warrant this afternoon and run up to Liverpool by to-night's train."

"Sit still a moment while I get Sir William's approval. The case is an important one."

Morden hurried down the passage to his Chief's room. He found Lorimer alone, and he recounted Richardson's story to him.

"I don't very much like the practice of arresting a man on a lesser charge in the hope of finding evidence to justify a charge of murder," said Lorimer, "but if ever there was a case where it was justified, this is it. It seems to me a very sound piece of work on the part of Richardson. I think you will agree with me now that his promotion out of his turn was justified. That young man will go far, you'll see."

"I think he will if he does not allow his zeal to outrun his discretion."

"The trouble with so many of our men is that they are so much afraid of the comments of the judges that they never give their zeal a chance. I don't mean that they should rush at their cases like a bull at a gate and go outside their legal powers, but sometimes they forget that their first duty is the protection of the public, and making crime an unprofitable profession. Certainly he should get a warrant, and be careful not to tread on the toes of the Liverpool force. They have a good C.I.D., and they will help him—especially if he takes a letter from me. Let me know the result."

Morden returned to his room. "I've told Sir William what you propose, and he approves, but he wants you to be careful to let the Liverpool C.I.D do most of the work themselves. He is going to give you a letter to the Chief Constable, and, meanwhile, slip down to Bow Street and swear your information. Have you written your report on what you did in France?"

"Yes, sir, it will reach you in a few minutes."

Richardson knew the routine at Bow Street very well. In half an hour he was in possession of the warrant and was back at New Scotland Yard for the letter. While he was waiting for it the messenger looked in.

"There's a gentleman in the hall asking for you, Inspector. He wouldn't give his name, but he has a little boy with him."

Richardson glanced at the clock in astonishment. It seemed impossible that his friends could have reached London in time for lunch after sleeping in Paris, but when he reached the hall and saw Jim Milsom and little Godfrey Maze beside him, dancing from one foot to the other with excitement, he understood. They had flown over from Le Bourget.

The boy came running to him. "We flew over," he shouted. "It's the first time I've ever been in an aeroplane, and Uncle Jim says that it won't be the last! It was such fun." He slipped his hand into Richardson's. "Uncle Jim says that you are to come and lunch with us. He told me to run and fetch you."

"All right, but I've got something to do with you first. I've got to take you to see a gentleman who's heard all about you."

He explained briefly to Jim Milsom what he proposed to do. "I should like my Chief to see this young man while he has the opportunity."

With Godfrey's hand in his he tapped at Morden's door.

"Come in," cried the weary voice.

"I'm sorry to interrupt you again, sir, but I thought that you might like to see the small boy we've brought back with us from France."

Godfrey Maze advanced to the table without any trace of embarrassment. Morden shook him by the hand.

"What a lot of books you've got on your table," exclaimed Godfrey, with wide eyes. "Are you learning French? I was until Uncle Jim came and took me away. These are English clothes, you know, and that makes me feel a real Englishman again."

Morden patted him on the head in fatherly fashion as an intimation that the interview was closed. As Richardson led him out he waved good-bye to his new acquaintance.

There was indeed no reason why Richardson should decline the invitation to lunch. Officially speaking, he was still on leave; he had all the necessary legal documents, and the railway warrant for his journey to Liverpool: he was perfectly free to spend the afternoon with his friends.

He shook hands with Jim Milsom and congratulated him on his quick journey from Paris. "Flying over was your idea, I suppose?"

"Why yes, I wanted to watch the face of this young nephew of mine as he left the ground. Like love it comes to a man only once in a lifetime, and I suppose that when he's grown up people will use planes just as they use cars in these days. Now, Inspector, my uncle insists on your lunching with us. He's taken a table at the Berkeley, and if we keep him any longer watching other people eat, he'll be ready to eat us."

The old man greeted him warmly and put him in the seat on his right. "You've been having a busy morning, Inspector, I guess. I hope that you found out all you wanted to?"

"Yes, Mr. Hudson, and I am very glad of your invitation to lunch because I have to leave for Liverpool to-night, and I might not have had an opportunity of thanking you for all your kindness before I went."

"The thanking ought to be all the other way. You've given me a wonderful time. Now I have a question to ask you and I'll put it now, before the waiter comes with the eats. It is about this boy. How do we stand in regard to him?"

"I don't quite know, sir. I have ascertained from an inspection of his father's will that he is heir to a considerable fortune from his father, but his guardian and trustee was his uncle, John Maze, and we don't know yet what has become of his money."

"You're going up to Liverpool to arrest him for murder?"

"No, sir--only for making a false attestation of that boy's death."

"Well, then, in any case he'll go to gaol and the boy will have no guardian. You'll find that the guy you're going to arrest has made away with the boy's money, and what then? Now I—I have an offer to make to the British authorities. I'll adopt the boy and treat him as my own son. What about that?"

"I don't think that we have any jurisdiction over what becomes of the boy. Probably the authorities will want to put him under the care of the Public Trustee, but I am no lawyer, Mr. Hudson."

"Well, then, how shall I set about it?"

"In your place I should go to a good solicitor in London and ask him to take up the case for you. I can give you the name of a thoroughly trustworthy firm, but in your place I should not take any step until you see how the case goes with John Maze."

Mr. Hudson showed his disappointment. "I thought that you folks could do anything you wanted to. A firm of lawyers will keep me hanging on and on, running up fees and doing not a thing for me in the end. I suppose," he added wistfully, "that you couldn't let me come up to Liverpool with you?"

"I'm afraid not, sir. Besides, you would see nothing. I shall be busy with the police all day to-morrow. But the man will be brought up before the magistrate at Bow Street the day after to-morrow, and you could be in court to hear the proceedings."

"Okay! I shall be there."

"And in the meantime, if you could look after the boy, either at your hotel, or at your nephew's flat..."

"I'll leave him with Jim. They've chummed up together."

"And of course you'll see that he isn't in court when Maze is being tried."

"Trust me for that. Ah! Here's our food at last."

During the meal Richardson related what had happened during his absence about Wilfred Bryant. They listened with interest, but already Bryant had slipped into the background of their minds.

"I suppose that this often happens in this work of yours, Inspector," observed Hudson. "While you're hunting one jack-rabbit the real guy pops up and leads you off in another direction altogether."

"Yes, sir, but if we get the real jack-rabbit in the end there's no harm done."

Richardson spent part of the afternoon with his friends and then, armed with the letter from his Chief and all the other necessary papers, he went to Euston and took the train to Liverpool. There was nothing to be done before ten o'clock next morning, but Richardson knew personally the inspector in charge of the C.I.D. staff and he determined to call upon him at nine.

At that hour he found himself in Dale Street, and was even stopped at the door by one of the gigantic constables who are the pride of Liverpool.

"The C.I.D., sir? First door to the right at the top of the stairs."

He was welcomed by the inspector as an old comrade. "What have you got for us to-day, Mr. Richardson?" he asked in a broad Lowland accent.

"I've a warrant for you to execute, Mr. Anstruther. Here it is."

As Anstruther read it wrinkles began to form on his forehead.

"Hey! but yon's one of the city magistrates and a solicitor, and you say he's sworn a false attestation..."

"Even magistrates are only human, Mr. Anstruther. I won't hide from you that a far graver charge may be brought against him after you've searched his house."

"Ah! I see. You're on a fishing excursion for evidence. Well, I'll no say that there haven't been stories about him here in Liverpool, but before executing this warrant and handing him over to you, I think that I should report to my Chief."

"I have a letter from the Commissioner to the Chief Constable—an open letter. Perhaps you will take it with you."

Inspector Anstruther glanced at the clock. "He'll no be in his room before ten. While we're waiting you might tell me what kind of evidence you'll be looking for in the search."

Richardson gave him a short résumé of the case.

"I see," said Anstruther; "but all this you've told me has nothing to do with the false attestation. I mean the question of the cigarette found in the woman's room and that postage-stamp."

"You may possibly find evidence showing that after obtaining possession of his nephew's property he converted it into his own use."

"Ay; I've heard some whisper of that kind about him, but a' that will take time."

"It will, but there's one thing that won't take time —to take his fingerprints when you get him down to Dale Street."

"You think he won't object as an untried prisoner?"

"Men of that class very seldom do. They think that refusal may prejudice their case."

"Ay, you're right about that."

"We shall want to put a few questions to that butler of his, to know whether his master was away from home on the night of May 15th."

"H'm! Butlers don't keep diaries as a rule, but we can try. I suppose you've got your evidence all cut and dried about the false attestation."

"He swore that to his knowledge the boy was dead. We can produce that boy, besides witnesses from France who can identify Maze."

"Very well. That's ten o'clock striking. I'll just run upstairs with this letter and get approval, then we'll start."

"I hope you'll come yourself, Mr. Anstruther."

"Indeed I will."

Five minutes later Anstruther came down. "It's a' right. I'm to go with you and take a couple of my best men, with two men in reserve outside in case they're needed." He became busy with his desk telephone.

One by one, four men made their appearance and stood to attention.

"Now listen," said their inspector. "This is Inspector Richardson from the Yard. He's brought a warrant for us to execute for the arrest of John Maze, one of the city magistrates."

The eyebrows were raised in blank astonishment. Anstruther continued, "We shall make the arrest at the house in Apsley Terrace and keep him in one of the rooms while we search the house. You, Sergeant Darley, will be in charge of him and ready to note down anything he says. The others will help in the search. Get your hats and we'll start."

When they arrived at the house in the placid and dignified suburb, Anstruther went to the door with Richardson and the others kept out of sight. Anstruther rang the bell and they were admitted.

"What name shall I give?" asked the butler.

"Inspector Anstruther from Dale Street."

"Very good, sir. If you will both take a seat I will ascertain whether Mr. Maze will see you."

Anstruther made a little signal to his companion unseen by the butler, and they followed him into the library as soon as the door was open. John Maze looked up from the desk where he was writing letters, and changed colour.

"You can step outside until you are wanted," said Anstruther to the butler, and he waited until the door was shut behind him. Maze had risen.

"I'm sorry, Mr. Maze, but I have here a warrant for your arrest, dated yesterday, from Bow Street. I will read it to you."

Maze listened to the text of the warrant in silence, then he said, "A ridiculous mistake has been made, but for that, of course, I can't blame you. You are only doing your duty. Does this mean that I am to be taken to London?"

"Yes, sir," said Richardson, "I shall be accompanying you."

"I've seen your face before. Didn't you call here about a fortnight ago?"

"Yes, sir, I did."

"We shall have to make a search of your house, Mr. Maze."

"Search the house! Do you take me for a receiver of stolen property?"

"No, sir; it is in compliance with the rule when warrants for felony are executed." He made a covert signal to Richardson who went out to call in the men.

They tramped into the hall and Anstruther called in Sergeant Darley. "Will you take this gentleman to a room upstairs: he is under arrest."

"This way, please, sir," said Darley, making Maze lead the way up the stairs. He glanced into two or three bedrooms and selected one in which the furniture was covered with dust sheets. There he told the prisoner to sit down.

Meanwhile, downstairs a systematic search was being made, while Richardson took the butler into the dining-room to ask him a question.

"Did Mr. Maze sleep here on the night of Tuesday, May 15th?"

"He very rarely spends the night away from home, sir. May 15th? That would be about a fortnight ago, wouldn't it? No, sir, he hasn't slept away from home for at least six weeks."

"Can you remember whether he was out on that Tuesday?"

The butler seemed to see a ray of light. "I remember now, sir; he was out to lunch and dinner that Tuesday and he didn't get home until after I went to bed, but that's not uncommon with him when he dines out for a bridge party. He was awake when I brought him his tea next morning."

Richardson sat down at the table and wrote this statement at full speed in his notebook. "Just put your name to that," he said, after reading the statement over to the man. He returned to the library and found Anstruther giving final instructions to the searching officers.

"So what you've got to look for is cigarettes and any kind of poison, which means any small bottle of liquid or packet of powder. Next, you've got to collect private papers, letters and so forth. We shall have to cart them all down to Dale Street to be gone through. Now get to work."

An idea occurred to Richardson. He called to the butler. "I suppose you've all kinds of cigarettes in the house?"

"No, sir, not all kinds. Mr. Maze is very particular about his cigarettes, especially those he carries on him and offers to his friends. I keep them under lock and key till he asks for them."

"You might let me have one."

"Certainly, sir." He took a bunch of keys from his pocket and opened a drawer in the dining-room. It was crammed with cigarette boxes. Richardson opened one, and there, with a beating heart, he found the fellows to the cigarette he had picked up in Naomi Clynes' bed-sitting-room. He slipped the box into his pocket and told his colleague Anstruther that cigarettes might be struck out of the list of searches.

In three-quarters of an hour the dining-room table was loaded with small bottles and paper packets of chemicals gathered from almost every room in the house, but principally from the drawers in the library and Maze's dressing-room upstairs.

"It's going to be a job to get all this stuff analysed," observed Anstruther.

"Where there are chemists' labels on the packets and the bottles the inquiry can be shortened. Chemists would be able to say off-hand what the stuff was. Hallo! What's this? Now we're getting warm. Look at this." He held up an odd-shaped little phial with a French label on it. "Dumont, Pharmacien, Orleans. I think we shall find that we need not go any further than this bottle. If you agree, Mr. Anstruther, I should like to take it up with me to London and get the Home Office analyst to vet it."

"Certainly, and what about all these papers?"

"Oh, I suppose that you can get them packed up and sent on to the Yard. We'll go through them there."

The two inspectors went upstairs while their men went in search of taxis. "Now, Mr. Maze," said Anstruther, "if you'll come downstairs..."

Richardson held Sergeant Darley back. "Did he say anything to you?"

"Nothing that was worth noting down. He seemed to want to know what was to be done with him and I told him that I didn't know."

Chapter Eighteen

THREE TAXIS had carried the party down to Dale Street. John Maze had been conducted to the Fingerprint Registry while Richardson waited below in the inspector's room. After a moment's demur the prisoner had submitted to having his prints taken. "All right," he had said; "I suppose that it's the usual formality." He was then lodged in a cell, while Anstruther rejoined his London colleague, who was waiting impatiently with a fingerprint form in his hand.

"Here you are, Mr. Richardson. Do you want a magnifier?"

Richardson scanned the prints without answering.

"Here! Look at this." He was pointing to the print of the forefinger of the right hand, and the little print he had brought with him which he laid beside the other. Anstruther compared them, breathing hard. "Ay! I should say that this print taken from the woman's typewriter will hang him. The two prints are as like as two peas. I suppose that he doesn't know that you've got that print?"

"No, and he won't know it before his trial. But we've more evidence than that against him—all circumstantial. It's true that his butler has signed a statement to the effect that his master was not away from home on the night when Miss Clynes was murdered."

"Apart from that is there enough, do you think, to satisfy the Director of Public Prosecutions?"

"That remains to be seen. Now will you give me the trains to Euston? I don't want to get in too late."

They consulted a time-table, and chose a train that reached Euston between six and seven. There was time to eat a scratch lunch before driving to the station, and at the appointed hour Richardson called at Dale Street for his prisoner and they drove down to the station together. The arrangement had run so smoothly that none of the local reporters had got wind of the arrest.

Richardson had arranged with the guard that they should have the compartment to themselves. His prisoner was disposed to be conversational. He seemed quite to have recovered his spirits. "It is funny meeting you up here again, Inspector," he said. "I suppose that you have a lot of running about to do?"

"Sometimes, Mr. Maze."

"I suppose that I shall be allowed to consult my solicitor when we get to London?"

"Certainly. If you tell me his name and address I will see that a message is sent to him in time for him to be in court to-morrow morning."

"Whittock is his name. He is the London agent of my solicitors in Liverpool, but I don't know his address."

Richardson made a note of the name, and promised to look up his address in the Law List and have a message sent to him in the morning.

A few minutes later Maze closed his eyes and seemed to be disposing himself to sleep. Richardson found himself wondering whether he would be able to drop off to sleep so easily if he was under the shadow of the gallows. This man had extraordinary nerve. In reality, however, Maze was only feigning sleep and was anxiously surveying his position.

The hours passed slowly, but at last the train was in the far-flung suburbs of North London and Maze appeared to wake up with a start. At Euston the two men attracted no attention with their modest hand-bags. They entered a taxi and Richardson gave the order to drive to Bow Street. The formalities to be complied with were short. He handed over his prisoner and the warrant to the officer in charge, and Maze was taken downstairs to the cells. Richardson asked leave to use the inspector's telephone to head-quarters and rang up Mr. Morden, knowing that during busy times, he was apt to stay in his office to a late hour. A familiar voice answered him.

"Inspector Richardson speaking from Bow Street, sir. I've lodged that man from Liverpool in the cells here. Could I see you if I came along at once?"

"Yes," was the answer. "I'll wait for you."

"Well, Mr. Richardson, you haven't been long away."

"No, sir, everything happened to go without a hitch. The Liverpool C.I.D. helped me very much; they made the arrest and their men did most of the searching. We took the prisoner's fingerprints at Dale Street and found that the print of the forefinger of the right hand was identical with that which was found on the spacing-bar of the typewriter."

"Come, you're getting on."

"Yes, sir, but I don't think we've yet got all we want. It's true I've brought back with me this bottle of fluid that has the label of a chemist in Orleans. It may prove to contain a poison or it may not."

"Right! We'll have it analysed."

"We brought back with us a sack full of papers, which will have to be examined."

"I don't see how you are likely to find any evidence of the murder in them, but they may have a bearing on the false attestation."

"Quite so, sir, but if you remember, the murderer took away quite a number of papers from Miss Clynes' room. He dropped some in the taxi, but her diary was missing, and probably other papers."

"I don't think that kind of man would keep incriminating papers, but go through them carefully by all means."

"I'm afraid that I must report one difficulty, sir. Maze's butler has made a statement that his master slept at home on May 15th, and so he will be a useful witness for the defence."

"Alibis are the devil in a case like this. Did the man appear to be speaking the truth as far as his memory went?"

"Yes, sir, he did, but I think that with a little extra work the alibi may be broken down. The butler says that he found his master in bed next morning, and does not know at what hour he came back. The cabman who we think took him nearly to Euston that night, was paid off between 10.30 and 11 p.m., in time to catch the midnight train. That train would not have got to Liverpool in time for the butler to find him in bed next morning."

"Well, then, perhaps the alibi is watertight."

"I think not, sir. After the remand to-morrow morning I'm going to make a tour of the garages in the neighbourhood of Euston. If he took a car at 11 p.m. he could have got home by 4 a.m.; a good car would average fifty miles an hour at night with no traffic."

"Well, I wish you luck, but I can't say that I feel altogether hopeful. You must see me again before taking the papers over to the Director of Public Prosecutions. Of course, you will apply for a week's remand to-morrow morning."

Richardson was out of bed at daybreak, running through the sackful of papers taken from his prisoner's house, It proved to be a vain quest as regards anything belonging to Miss Clynes, but he put aside a bank passbook and a number of brokers' notes that seemed at first sight to suggest that Maze had been converting trust money to his own use. His watch lay before him on the table, and he saw that if he was to get to Bow Street in time, a further search must be deferred.

At Bow Street the case was called on. The prisoner came into the dock from the cells below, and a lawyer rose in the body of the court to say that he represented the prisoner. Richardson was called and gave evidence of the arrest, asking for a remand of eight days. The prisoner's lawyer applied for bail; this Richardson formally opposed, and when pressed for his reason, stated that the prisoner had lately been abroad, and that there were special reasons why the application should be refused.

"Really, your Worship," objected the lawyer, "this is going too far. My client is a magistrate; he is quite ready to meet the charge and to prove his innocence, and it would prejudice his defence if he was not admitted to bail."

"If the police oppose bail, I cannot grant it at this stage," said the magistrate.

Richardson was now free to hunt for evidence that would outweigh the alibi. He went methodically to work by making a list from the post office directory of every garage within a radius of a mile from Euston Station. It was a formidable list, but he did not dare to entrust it to detective officers in the division concerned, in case an inquiry should be perfunctory. "If you want a thing well done, do it yourself," was his motto.

After six failures and the loss of a good two hours, he came upon what he wanted in a garage situated to the north of Euston Station, whose proprietor remembered receiving an unusual order from an unknown customer.

"I wasn't here myself at the time. My night-watchman received the order. He told me next morning that the gentleman was very insistent on hiring a car to take him to Liverpool. My man told him that the garage was closed for the night, and even if a car was available, there was no driver on the premises. The gentleman was just going away when one of our cars came in. The watchman told the driver what he'd been saying, and said, 'I don't suppose you feel like taking your car two hundred miles and back?'

"'I don't,' said the driver. Then the gentleman seems to have offered him five pounds for himself for the double journey, and that fixed it. The usual mileage for the car and five pounds extra for the driver."

"Can you get hold of the driver?"

"He's somewhere about the place now. George!" he shouted. A man emerged from behind a line of cars and came forward. "This is the man; ask him what you like."

"It's about that gentleman you drove to Liverpool on the night of May 15th. You remember it?"

"Yes, I remember it. Funny sort of gentleman he was. First he got up beside me and kept jumping up and down as if he thought it would make the car go faster. I had to tell him that he was interfering with my driving, so then he told me to pull up and he'd get inside. After that I had no trouble with him until we got to Liverpool at half-past four in the morning. Then he got at me again through the speaking-tube, hollering 'next to the right,' 'next to the left.' I tell you I was getting fed up with him. We'd got out into a street of houses standing in their own gardens and suddenly he yelled 'Stop!' I pulled up sharp and he got out with a big bundle of papers, paid me, and said 'thank you,' and walked away down a side street."

"Did you notice the time exactly?"

"Yes, it was twenty-five minutes past four."

"What did he look like?"

"I couldn't see him very well by lamplight. He was a tall man, between fifty and sixty, I should say."

"Do you think you would know him again if you saw him?"

"I might."

"Thank you. Will you give me your name and address in case you are wanted?"

"George Warner, 32 Forest Gate."

Richardson returned to New Scotland Yard feeling that, now that the alibi was broken, his task was nearly done. He had only to get the case for the prosecution down in writing, and his Chief would authorize him to take it over to the office of the Director of Public Prosecutions. The messenger stopped him in the hall.

"A gentleman has been ringing you up at intervals for the last half-hour. He wouldn't give his name—only his number. He said I was to be sure to ring him up as soon as you came in. Here's his number."

Richardson rang up the number, and a voice that he recognized replied in excited tones, "James Milsom speaking. Is that you, Inspector? Look here, I must see you on a very urgent matter. Can I see you now if I come down?"

"Certainly. No bad news, I hope?"

"That depends on what you call bad news. You'll have a shock, I can promise you that. I'll come right away."

Richardson's usually calm demeanour was shaken. He had a terrifying premonition that the boy, Godfrey Maze, had been lost, or had been run over by a taxi. He had to wait a full ten minutes under this awful fear before the door opened to admit Jim Milsom, for once serious and anxious-looking.

Richardson sprang up from his chair to shake hands with him. "Has anything happened to that little boy? Please tell me quickly."

Milsom stopped short in blank astonishment, and then burst out laughing. "Is that what you thought it was? I'm so sorry that I pulled your leg. No, the boy is all right. The shock I'm going to give you is of quite another kind. Last night I brought that poor woman's last manuscript home to read. I had just come to the last page and had turned it over when I saw writing on the back. I've brought it down with me for you to read and see what you can make out of it." He pulled a quarto sheet from his pocket. It was not typed, but written in pencil, with a few corrections, as if it was the draft of a letter. Richardson read it with growing excitement.

"DEAR MR. MAZE,

"For some weeks I have had something on my mind. Just before I left your service a letter came for you from France. The address was written in a childish hand, which I felt sure that I recognized as that of your dear little nephew. I took it in to you, feeling sure that you would tell me that the little boy whom you were mourning as dead, had somehow escaped from that dreadful railway accident on Christmas Eve, and that you had without knowing it buried another little boy in his stead. I remembered reading that some of the children were terribly mangled and that some of them were quite unrecognizable. But you said nothing about the letter, and afterwards I found in the wastepaper basket, the envelope torn up. I saved the stamp and the postmark from them, and I have them still. The thing is preying on my mind. It is so awful to think of that dear little boy being among strangers, not knowing a word of the language or how to get to his friends. There may, of course, be some quite natural explanation. If there is, I do hope you will send it to me and forgive me for having troubled you on a matter which, you may say, did not concern me. My excuse is that on the rare occasions when you brought him down to the office, he used to play with my typewriter, and we became great friends.

"Sincerely yours,

"NAOMI CLYNES."

"Do you recognize the handwriting, Mr. Milsom?"

"I could swear to it anywhere. Miss Clynes often wrote to me about her books, and I have kept her letters."

"Of course this pencil draft is not evidence that the letter was ever written, or that Maze ever received it, but dated as it is on

May 10th, the presumption is that the letter reached him. Its importance lies in the fact that it is the first time we have proof of a motive for the murder."

"That is what I thought. Of course the poor woman never knew that the draft of her letter had not been destroyed. This was the last page of her manuscript. She caught it up and shoved it into her machine without noticing that there was writing on the back. I've often done that myself, and probably you've done the same thing."

"You'll let me keep this sheet, sir?"

"Of course. That's why I brought it down. Now tell me how you are getting on with the case. Will you be able to hang this swine, Maze?"

"We are getting on all right, but it needs a bold man to say what the lawyers will decide, and still more to predict what a jury may do. Now, if you'll excuse me, Mr. Milsom, I must rush off. There is a lot to do to-day."

Charles Morden was not expected back from lunch until half-past two. Richardson munched a sandwich at his table while he wrote his report on the result of his inquiries of the morning, and on the draft of Miss Clynes' letter to Maze. The examination of the sack of documents brought away from the house in Liverpool had been entrusted to Sergeant Williams, who had had long practice in sifting the grain from the chaff in going through masses of documents. Richardson looked into the detective sergeant's room and found him at work at the big oak table. "Any luck?" he asked.

"I'm getting on, sir. So far I've found a number of letters showing that Maze has been for years embezzling trust funds, and that the beneficiaries have been getting restive. Things were just coming to a head when his nephew was killed in that accident in France, and he succeeded to his property. Since then he seems to have been using the money to pay back into the trust funds what he stole from them."

"So there's not much left?"

"I can't say that yet—not until I've been carefully through his passbooks from the bank, but by the day after tomorrow I hope to be able to produce a fairly accurate balance sheet."

"Have you come across any private letters—a letter signed Naomi Clynes, for instance?"

"No private letters at all, so far."

The messenger looked in. "Mr. Morden has just come in. He's alone for the moment."

Richardson hurried off to his Chief's room.

"Back already, Mr. Richardson?"

"Yes, sir, and I think that I've found enough to break down that alibi." He related what he had discovered at the garage. Morden nodded his head with satisfaction.

"And a friend of mine has brought me this." He laid Naomi Clynes' pencilled draft on the table.

"The draft of a letter, eh? But you haven't found the actual letter among the prisoner's papers?"

"No, sir, not yet. Sergeant Williams is searching for it. The gentleman who gave me this is prepared to swear to the handwriting."

Morden sighed. "All that this amounts to is that if we could put it in as evidence, it would suggest a motive for the crime, but I doubt very much whether we can use it, so it comes to this— that your case for the murder charge is as complete as you can make it. I'll initial your report and you had better take it over personally to the Director of Public Prosecutions."

"Very good, sir."

Richardson knew the routine at the office of the Director, which was staffed by a number of sound criminal lawyers, most of whom had practised in the Criminal Courts. He delivered his file of papers to the messenger who carried them to the room of the Assistant Director. Ten minutes later he was sent for. This official, a man of middle age with a cold eye, asked him whether he was the officer who had conducted the inquiries personally, and learning that he was, he said, "I must congratulate you, Inspector. I wish that all the police reports that are brought here were as clear as this. I've only had time to skim through the evidence, and I wish that it was a bit stronger as regards the murder charge. The other is, of course, capable of proof up to the hilt. I see here that you have recovered the little boy who this rascal swore had been killed. We may have to produce him in court. Now, the Assizes at the Central Criminal Court begin the week after next, and if we are going to charge this man with murder, it would be better not to keep him hanging about until the next Assizes, but to wipe the slate clean. It will mean a rush."

"It will, sir, but with all submission I think that the evidence ought to be sufficient—the fingerprint, the cigarette, and the knowledge which the accused had that the murdered woman knew that the little nephew was still alive."

"Yes, but that pencilled draft could not be put in, I'm afraid, without proof that the accused received it. Still, I think that we can risk it. The charge can always be dropped at a later stage if we encounter a snag. You say here that the man is in custody on remand until next Tuesday. Yes, I think that you may charge him."

"Very good, sir."

Richardson covered the ground back to Scotland Yard at his best speed. He sought an interview with Morden as soon as he had written out a short report of his interview with the Assistant Director, and asked him for written approval. This form of the traditional Scottish caution prevailed throughout the Department. High officials might have short memories about the verbal instructions that they give from time to time, but the written word is there to remind them.

"I have one piece of good news for you," said Morden. "Sir Gerald Whitcombe has made an analysis of the liquid in that bottle with the label of a French chemist in Orleans. You will remember that the bottle was labelled 'Poison' on a red label. It contained tincture of aconitina. That ought to strengthen our case."

Richardson's next resort was to Brixton prison to which all trial and remand prisoners in London are sent. For this expedition he had to take with him Sergeant Williams, who could be produced as a witness to anything which the prisoner might say in reply to the charge.

To the gatekeeper of that establishment he explained that he had been sent to read to the prisoner, John Maze, an additional charge that would be made against him at the next hearing. The gatekeeper spoke a few words on the telephone and let his visitor into the Central Hall where the chief warder awaited him.

"You want to see John Maze, Inspector?"

"Yes, I have to charge him with wilful murder."

"Have you? Does he expect it?"

"I fancy not."

"Well, if you'll take a seat in the adjudication room," said the chief warder, unlocking the door, "I'll have him brought down to you."

Two minutes later the door was thrown open and John Maze, followed by an assistant warder and the chief warder entered the room. He looked careworn and thinner and older than he did when Richardson had last seen him, and there was a curious air of fatalistic indifference about his bearing. He was wearing his own clothes.

"John Maze, I have been sent to read to you an additional charge which you will have to answer at the next hearing of your case. You are charged with the wilful murder of Naomi Clynes at 37A Seymour Street, Chelsea, on the evening of May 15th last. I have to caution you that you are not obliged to say anything, but that anything you do say will be taken down in writing and may be used against you at your trial."

The prisoner's behaviour was unusual. A fit of coughing seized him; he put his handkerchief to his mouth. There was a moment's pause, and then he caught at the back of an empty chair, staggered backwards and fell with the chair on top of him. As he was falling a strident laugh escaped his lips. He tried to speak but could not.

The chief warder put a whistle to his lips and shouted for the medical officer, but when that official came and the man was carried to the infirmary it was too late: he had passed to a higher tribunal than the Central Criminal Court.

Richardson waited in the prison to hear the doctor's pronouncement. The chief warder brought it to him.

"He must have had a tablet of cyanide of potassium in his handkerchief," he said. "Bad searching in the reception."

The death of John Maze left little Godfrey quite alone in the world. As events proved, very little of his fortune remained, and it was no doubt this factor that weighed with the court when it decided to grant to James Hudson, though an American citizen, the guardianship of the boy, an arrangement which made them both happy.

THE END